学术顾问

（以姓氏笔画为序）

王　宏　冯智文　李正栓　李丽生　原一川

Academic Advisors

Wang Hong　Feng Zhiwen　Li Zhengshuan

Li Lisheng　Yuan Yichuan

主　编

李昌银

副主编

黄　瑛　彭庆华

General Editor

Li Changyin

Professor of English　Yunnan Normal University

Associate General Editors

Huang Ying

Professor of English　Yunnan Normal University

Peng Qinghua

Professor of English　Yunnan Normal University

云南少数民族经典作品英译文库
Classics of Yunnan Ethnic Groups in English Translation

主编 李昌银 General Editor Li Changyin
副主编 黄瑛 彭庆华 Associate General Editors Huang Ying & Peng Qinghua

Mupamipa

牡帕密帕

搜集◎昆明师范学院中文系一九五七级部分学生
整理◎刘辉豪
英译◎李昌银
译校◎[美]包琼

Collected by the Class of 1961,
Department of Chinese, Kunming Teacher's College
Edited by Liu Huihao
Translated by Li Changyin
Revised by Joan Cecile Boulerice

云南出版集团
云南人民出版社

图书在版编目（CIP）数据

牡帕密帕 ： 汉、英 / 刘辉豪整理 ； 李昌银英译
. -- 昆明 ： 云南人民出版社，2020.2
（云南少数民族经典作品英译文库 / 李昌银主编）
ISBN 978-7-222-19071-9

Ⅰ. ①牡… Ⅱ. ①刘… ②李… Ⅲ. ①拉祜族－神话
－中国－汉、英 Ⅳ. ①I277.5

中国版本图书馆CIP数据核字(2020)第028262号

出 品 人 李 维 赵石定
项目统筹 周 祥 殷筱钊
项目组稿 郭木玉
责任编辑 郭木玉 阳 帆
装帧设计 马 滨 石 斌
责任校对 明 珍 李凯文 费 珺 溥 思
责任印制 陆卫华 代隆参

云南少数民族经典作品英译文库
Classics of Yunnan Ethnic Groups in English Translation

牡帕密帕
Mupamipa

搜集◎昆明师范学院中文系一九五七级部分学生
整理◎刘辉豪
英译◎李昌银
译校◎［美］包琼
Collected by the Class of 1961, Department of Chinese, Kunming Teacher's College
Edited by Liu Huihao
Translated by Li Changyin
Revised by Joan Cecile Boulerice

出 版 云南出版集团 云南人民出版社
发 行 云南人民出版社
社 址 昆明市环城西路609号
邮 编 650034
网 址 www.ynpph.com.cn
E-mail ynrms@sina.com
开 本 787mm×1092mm 1/16
印 张 11.5
字 数 156千
版 次 2020年2月第1版第1次印刷
印 刷 云南出版印刷集团有限责任公司 云南新华印刷一厂
书 号 ISBN 978-7-222-19071-9
定 价 60.00元

云南人民出版社
微信公众号

序　一

◎李正栓

民族典籍英译是传播中国文化、文学和文明的重要途径，是中华文化走出去的重要组成部分。文化与文学的传播，是一个国家提高文化软实力的重要方式，在文化交流和文明建设中起着不可或缺的作用，对提高国家对外话语权、构建国家对外话语体系以及对建设世界文学都有积极意义。

中国各少数民族拥有许多优秀的典籍，具有很高的文物价值、文学价值和文化价值。各民族的先人们通过口头流传或用文字记述了他们各具特色的文化。各少数民族几乎都有自己民族的创世史、史诗和神话传说。

中国民族典籍独具特色，不可替代。重视民族典籍的翻译和研究工作，对于挖掘各民族优秀文化，保护各民族文明，增强各民族之间的沟通和了解，进一步向世界其他地区传播各少数民族优秀文化，乃至提高我国文化软实力都有着重要意义。不少少数民族聚居地处于祖国边疆，有的处在“一带一路”建设关键部位，有的处在与周边国家进行各种交流的重要位置。

中国民族典籍是世界多元文化的有机组成部分，与其他文化共同造就了世界文化的绚丽多姿。世界正因为其文化多样性才变得缤纷多彩。我国各民族典籍中包含的文化多样性极大地丰富了世界多元、特色鲜明的文化。人们对多样性形成全新的认识角度和思维方式。多样性开阔了人们的视野，丰富了人们思考问题的角度。挖掘这些典籍中所蕴含的教育价值和文化价值，对世界其他民族都有指导和借鉴意义，并且有助于建设我国的文化自信。

民族典籍本身蕴含的特殊价值对加强民族文化了解、促进中外文化交流具有重大意义。民族典籍英译具有文学翻译和文化传递之功能，有对外宣传作用，还是一种文学外交。因此，民族典籍翻译和研究对于维护祖国统一、促进民族团结、稳定边疆以及增强国内各民族和中外文化之间的交流都起着极为重要的作用。

中华人民共和国成立以后，中央政府一直十分重视民族典籍翻译和研究工作，提供了强有力的政策支持，并采取了一系列有效措施，加快了各少数民族典籍的抢救、整理、翻译和研究的进程。中央政府多次召开西藏工作会议和新疆工作会议。近年来，国际和国内对于多元文化高度关注，少数民族文学典籍的翻译已然成为业内研究的热点。

近年来，民族典籍翻译和研究迅猛发展，势头良好。国家大力支持，发放国家社科基金课题，教育部和国家民委也发放课题，扶持了一大批研究者。很多民族典籍翻译课题得以立项并顺利开展；为数不少的民族典籍被翻译成汉语、英语和其他语言并出版发行；越来越多的业界人士致力于这个满富生机的学术领域。

在中国文化走出去的国家战略下，全国少数民族典籍英译学术研讨会陆续召开，已经召开三次。

云南是中国民族最多的省份。人口在5000人以上的少数民族有25个，其中有15个民族为云南所特有，分别是：白族、哈尼族、傣族、傈僳族、佤族、拉祜族、纳西族、景颇族、布朗族、普米族、阿昌族、基诺族、怒族、德昂族、独龙族。其中除白族人口占全国白族人口总数的84%以上外，其他14个民族95%居住在云南。

云南还是我国跨境民族最多的省份。在云南的25个少数民族中，有16个民族跨境而居，分别是：傣族、壮族、苗族、景颇族、瑶族、哈尼族、德昂族、佤族、拉祜族、彝族、阿昌族、傈僳族、布依族、怒族、布朗族、独龙族。

云南少数民族创造了辉煌的文化。据不完全统计，云南少数民族文字文献古籍蕴藏量达10万余册（卷），口传古籍4万余种。云南省民委少数民族古籍整理出版规划办公室为了挽救和保护这些古籍，计划在5年内编纂出版100卷《云南少数民族古籍珍本集成》。这是一个令人瞩目的庞大计划。将这些古籍中的珍品翻译介绍给世界，不仅能够弘扬云南省丰富多彩的民族文化，而且有助于增进与南亚东南亚国家的理解与交流，为“一带一路”倡议的实施做出贡献。

云南师范大学外国语学院很重视这一领域的工作。在外国语学院领导支持下，李昌银教授带领一个由教授和中青年学者组成的团队对精选出来的17部云南少数民族经典作品进行英译，计划在5年内（“十三五”期间）翻译出版。这是一项十分有意义的宏大工程。

这17部民族典籍，内容全部为各民族的英雄史诗或神话传说，具有很高的历史意义和文学价值。这些作品涉及阿昌族、白族、傣族、德昂族、哈尼族、景颇族、拉祜族、苗族、纳西族、普米族、彝族等 11 个少数民族。

云南师范大学这支翻译队伍实力强大，主要由一些多年从事翻译教学、研究和实践的教授和副教授组成，他们是李昌银、黄瑛、彭庆华、孙兴文、吴相如、刘德周、杨慧芳、郜菊、陈萍、包琼（Joan Cecile Boulerice）等国内外专家学者。他们在云南翻译界都是风云人物。

在民族典籍英译中，这支队伍异军突起，为我国民族典籍英译壮大了声势，必将为中国民族典籍走向世界而成为世界文学的一部分做出新贡献。

民族典籍翻译与研究事业关乎国家的稳定统一，关乎民族关系的和谐发展，关乎世界多元文化的实现。在中国，民族典籍资源极为丰富，有待进一步挖掘、翻译。因此，民族典籍英译前景光明。同时，我们也应意识到，仍有许多濒临消失的少数民族典籍亟待拯救，民族典籍翻译与研究工作任重而道远。

（李正栓，中国英汉语比较研究会典籍英译专业委员会常务副会长兼秘书长、河北师范大学博士生导师）

Foreword by Li Zhengshuan

The translation of Chinese ethnic classics is an important approach in spreading Chinese culture, literature and civilization. It is a crucial component of Chinese culture going global. The spreading of Chinese culture and literature is a national policy and an important way to improve the cultural soft power of China. It plays an indispensable role in the cultural exchange between China and other countries and the development of world literature.

The ethnic groups in China have countless excellent classics with high anthropological, literary and cultural value. The ancestors of each ethnic group have passed down their distinctive culture orally or in writing. Almost all the ethnic groups have their own story of creation, epics, myths and legends.

Chinese ethnic classics are unique and irreplaceable. It is imperative to attach importance to the translation and research of ethnic classics; to explore the excellent ethnic cultures; to protect the civilization of ethnic groups; to enhance the communication and understanding among ethnic groups; to further spread the outstanding culture of ethnic groups to other parts of the world; and to build the cultural strength of China. Many ethnic groups live in the border areas and thus play an important role in the cultural and economic cooperation between China and its neighbors in the context of the Belt and Road Initiative.

Chinese ethnic classics are an important component of the magnificence and diversity of world culture. It is diversity that makes the world so colorful. The cultural diversity of Chinese ethnic classics has greatly enriched the world's pluralism and its distinctive features. People around the world have formed a new understanding of diversity. This diversity has expanded people's horizon and enriched their way of thinking. Digging out the educational and cultural value in these classics can contribute to the construction of China's self-confidence in culture.

The special value of the ethnic classics itself is of great significance to the strengthening of national culture and intercultural communication between China and foreign countries. The translation of ethnic classics is not just a literary exchange, but also a form of cultural communication. It is diplomacy through literature in that it consolidates the cultural ties between China and other countries.

After the founding of the People's Republic of China, the central government attached great importance to the translation and research of ethnic classics, provided a great deal of policy support, and adopted a series of effective measures to speed up the process of rescuing, collating, translating and studying ethnic classics. The central government has convened several working conferences on Tibet and Xinjiang. In recent years, both China and other countries have paid close attention to multiculture. The translation of ethnic classics has become a hot topic.

In recent years, the translation and research of ethnic classics have progressed rapidly and have shown good prospects. The government strongly supports and grants the research projects of the national social science fund. The Ministry of Education and the State Ethnic Affairs Commission are also issuing research projects and giving funding to a large number of researchers. Many research projects on ethnic classics have been approved and carried out. Many ethnic classics have been translated into Chinese, English and other languages and published. More and more professionals have dedicated themselves to this new sphere of learning.

In this context, the academic conferences on translation of ethnic classics are held one after another all around the country. And up to now three have been held.

Yunnan is the province which has the most ethnic groups in China. Besides the Han people, there are 25 ethnic groups, each with a population of more than 5,000. Among them, 15 ethnic groups are unique to Yunnan, which are the Bai, the Hani, the Dai, the Lisu, the Wa, the Lahu, the Naxi, the Jingpo, the Bulang, the Pumi, the Achang, the Jinuo, the Nu, the De'ang and the Dulong. Among these, 84% of the total number of the Bai people in China and 95% of the other 14 ethnic groups are living in Yunnan.

Yunnan is also the province which has the most cross-border ethnic groups. Of the 25 ethnic groups, 16 live across the border, namely: the Dai, the Zhuang, the Miao, the Jingpo, the Yao, the Hani, the De'ang, the Wa, the Lahu, the Yi, the Achang, the Lisu, the Buyi, the Nu, the Bulang and the Dulong.

The ethnic groups in Yunnan have created splendid cultures. According to statistics, the number of classics of Yunnan ethnic groups is more than 100 thousand volumes and classics in oral tradition are more than 40 thousand. In order to save and protect these ancient books, the Office of Classics Collation and Publishing of Yunnan Ethnic Groups Affairs Commission planned to compile and publish 100 volumes of *A Collection of Yunnan Ethnic Group Rare Books* in five years, which is an ambitious plan. The introduction of the ancient classics via translation can not only promote and develop the colorful ethnic cultures of Yunnan, but also contribute to the understanding and exchange between China and countries in South Asia and Southeast Asia and to the implementation of the Belt and Road Initiative as well.

The School of Foreign Languages and Literature of Yunnan Normal University is paying close attention to this field. With the support of the School and the University,

Professor Li Changyin is leading a group of professors and young scholars to do the project of *Classics of Yunnan Ethnic Groups in English Translation*, which includes 17 ethnic classics selected carefully from Yunnan's bountiful ethnic classics. These books are the heroic epics or myths and legends of each ethnic groups with great historical significance and literary value. They will finish the translation in five years (during the Thirteenth Five-Year Plan). After that, all the works will be published by Yunnan People's Publishing House.

The 17 works cover 11 ethnic groups: the Achang, the Bai, the Dai, the De'ang, the Hani, the Jingpo, the Lahu, the Miao, the Naxi, the Pumi and the Yi. All of these groups except the Miao and the Yi are unique to Yunnan.

The translation team of Yunnan Normal University is full of strength and vitality, composed of professors and associate professors who have been occupied in translation teaching, research, and practice for a long time. They are Li Changyin, Huang Ying, Peng Qinghua, Sun Xingwen, Wu Xiangru, Liu Dezhou, Yang Huifang, Gao Ju, Chen Ping, Joan Boulerice and other experts and scholars who are representative figures in the translation field in Yunnan province.

This team is a new force that has suddenly arisen in terms of translating ethnic classics. It is expanding the momentum of ethnic classics translation in China and has made a new contribution for China's ethnic classics to go global and become a part of world literature.

The translation and research of ethnic classics are related to the development of Chinese culture and the realization of multiculturalism in the world. In China, ethnic classics are extremely rich in resources, which require us to make further exploration and research and translate them into other languages. Therefore, the future of translating ethnic classics is bright. At the same time, we should also realize that there are still many ethnic works which are close to extinction and urgently need to be rescued. We still have a long way to go in the fields of translation and research in ethnic classics.

(Li Zhengshuan, Standing Vice Chairman and Secretary General, Classics Translation Committee of CACSEC, PhD supervisor at Hebei Normal University)

序　二

◎王　宏

好友云南师范大学外国语学院李昌银教授来电嘱托我为“云南少数民族经典作品英译文库”的出版写一序言，并随即发来该文库的背景资料，让我“不着急，慢慢写”。我本人从事中国典籍英译及研究，深知少数民族典籍对外传译的重要性，但又是少数民族典籍翻译的门外汉。因此，我是怀着虚心学习的态度来写此序言的。近年来，在中国文化“走出去”战略工程大背景下，在中央和地方各级政府的大力支持下，我国少数民族典籍的对外传译及研究工作顺利开展，取得了很大的进步。请看以下数据：

2008 年，广西百色学院韩家权教授获批国家社科基金项目《布洛陀史诗》（壮汉英对照）。该项目已顺利结项，并于 2013 年 12 月获得中国民间文艺最高奖“山花奖”。

2012 年，广西百色学院外语系翻译团队翻译的国家级非物质文化遗产《壮族嘹歌》（英文版）由广西师范大学出版社正式出版。

2012 年，东北大学秦皇岛分校吴松林教授主编的《蒙古族系列：江格尔（汉英对照）》（上下册）由吉林大学出版社出版。

2013 年，河北师范大学李正栓教授英译《藏族格言诗》

由长春出版社出版发行。

2013 年，云南财经大学崔晓霞教授撰写的《〈阿诗玛〉英译研究》收入由王宏印教授主编、民族出版社出版的“民族典籍翻译研究丛书”。

2014 年，东北大学秦皇岛分校吴松林教授撰写的《满族档案文献研究》申请到国家社科后期资助，他英译的《英雄格斯尔可汗》由吉林大学出版社出版。

2014 年，中南民族大学张立玉教授主持的“土家族主要典籍英译及研究”获批国家社科基金项目。

2015 年，西安外国语大学梁真惠副教授撰写的《〈玛纳斯〉翻译传播研究》收入由王宏印教授主编、民族出版社出版的“民族典籍翻译研究丛书”。

与此同时，第一届和第二届全国少数民族典籍英译学术研讨会分别于 2012 年和 2014 年在广西民族大学和大连民族学院举行，参加会议的院校分布之广、与会代表数量之众、提交论文数量之多和涉及研究话题之细，十分可喜。2016 年还将在中南民族大学举行第三届全国少数民族典籍英译学术研讨会。

为什么少数民族典籍的对外传译及研究工作在短短几年就受到译界的青睐，取得众多成果？我认为，这在很大程度上归于典籍翻译界乃至翻译界同仁对“中国典籍”的重新思考和认识。中国典籍浩如烟海，卷帙浩繁，举世瞩目，是全人类共同的精神财富。但对于中国典籍的理解，我们以前较多限于汉民族的重要文献和书籍，而对少数民族多有忽略。在讨论中国典籍时，也较多关注古代文学作品。其实，中国典籍指“中国清代末年1911年以前的重要文献和书籍”，这就要求我们从事典籍翻译时，不但要翻译古代文学典籍作品，还要翻译古代哲学、科技、法律、医学、经济、军事、天文、地理等诸多方面的典籍作品，不但要翻译汉民族的典籍作品，也要翻译各少数民族的典籍作品。

民族典籍具有该民族的原型符号的特质，蕴藏着能够“遗传”并不断“再生”的文化基因。民族典籍是中华传统文化的内核，同时还是中华传统文化的符号构成规则。中国是具有56个民族的多民族国家，少数民族典籍是我国少数民族勤劳与智慧的结晶，是中华文明、也是世界文明不可或缺的一部分。少数民族典籍对外传译具有跨文化交流的作用，它不但有助于更多的人了解少数民族的独特文化，而且还有助于保护少数民族文化的独特性、维持少数民族文化多样性、促进各民族团结、提升中华文化软实力等。

中国少数民族典籍涉及宗教、文学、历史、语言、医学、天文历算等领域，内容丰富，版本多样，载体特殊，传承奇特。仅以《中国少数民族古籍总目提要》为例，该书于1997年正式立项，全书总体设计约60卷、110册，目前已出版23个民族卷共20册：纳西族卷、白族卷、东乡族卷·裕固族卷·保安族卷、土族卷·撒拉族卷、锡伯族卷、哈尼族卷、回族卷·铭刻、柯尔克孜族卷、羌族卷、毛南族卷·京族卷、仫佬族卷、达斡尔族卷、土家族卷、鄂温克族卷、鄂伦春族卷、赫哲族卷、苗族卷、侗族卷、黎族卷、朝鲜族卷。该书真实地反映了我国各少数民族古籍赋存的全面情况，充实了中国的历史和文化内容，为后人探索各种文化形式的源流、揭示中国社会文化发展的轨迹提供了极为珍贵的资料，为我国乃至世界各国人文科学研究提供了一套新颖而全面的资料，对于弘扬中华民族传统文化具有深远的历史意义和现实意义。

少数民族典籍的对外传译是一项艰巨的工作，涉及将少数民族语言译成汉语、少数民族语言之间的互译和少数民族语言译成外语（主要是英语）。前两类翻译历史源远流长，最早可追溯到春秋战国时代《越人歌》的翻译，即汉、壮语之间的翻译。少数民族典籍译成外语的时间则要晚一些。据考证，维吾尔族古典长诗《福乐智慧》成书于1069年或1070年，目前尚未发现完整的原稿，只存留下来三个抄本，分别为赫拉特抄本、费尔干纳抄本与埃及抄本，其中费尔干纳抄本于12~13世纪用阿拉伯文纳斯赫体抄写，1914年发现于今中亚乌孜别克斯坦纳曼干城，现存于该共和国科学院东方研究所。这是少数民族典籍译介到国外的最早纪录。少数民族典籍外译在现代有了较快发展。一些少数民族典籍，如藏族的《格萨尔王传》、蒙古族的《江格尔》和柯尔克孜族的《玛纳斯》等英雄史诗，云南彝族的《阿诗玛》、维吾尔族的《艾里甫和赛乃姆》等民间叙事长诗已先后被翻译成英语及其他外国文字，为世人所知。这对传承少数民族经典，推动中外文化交流起到了不可替代的作用。然而，还有大量的中国少数民族典籍等待我们去翻译和研究。

云南省少数民族典籍资源十分丰富。据不完全统计，云南少数民族文字文献古籍蕴藏量达10万余册（卷），口传古籍4万余种。“云南少数民族经典作品英译文库”正是依托云南省丰富的少数民族典籍资源，借助云南师范大学外国语学院强大的翻译师资队伍，在云南人民出版社的有力支持下，首次将云南少数民族经典作品成系列对外译介的大力举措。云南师范大学外国语学院对“云南少数民族经典作品英译文库”十分重视，他们首先邀请省内外少数民族语言文化研究专家对云南民族典籍和民族文化经典作品进行筛选，做到“好中选好，优中选优”，同时调配最强的翻译力量承担文库的翻译任务。我粗略看了该文库的选题，发现选题面广，覆盖范围宽，收入了云南省阿昌族、白族、傣族、纳西族、德昂族、哈尼族、景颇族、拉祜族、苗族、普米族和彝族等民族的典籍作品。云南共有25个少数民族，其中11个少数民族的典籍作品都覆盖到了，不少作品还是首次译成英文。这将彻底改变云南少数民族典籍由于对外译介数量较少，不为世界了解的尴尬局面。

对于云南师范大学外国语学院而言，把少数民族典籍英译作为翻译专业的优势特色进行建设，这将对该院的学科建设起到助推作用。“云南少数民族经典作品英译文库”所产生的翻译成果和研究成果将培养出一批优秀的典籍翻译和研究团队，凸显该院在全国的学术特色和学术影响，同时还能将翻译能力和研究能力转化为教学能力，提高云南师范大学外国语学院翻译专业研究生的培养质量，为社会输送高水平的翻译人才，有力地支撑学院翻译专业学科的建设和发展。我对云南师范大学外国语学院的翻译师资队伍较为熟悉。作为云南省唯一获得省级高校优势特色学科建设项目的外国语学院，该院具有雄厚的翻译师资力量，在云南省各高校中当属第一。多年来，该院翻译与跨文化研究团队一直承担着对外交流与合作的各种口笔译项目及任务。由外国语学院精心挑选和确定的“云南少数民族经典作品英译文库”翻译人员绝大多数都是云南省翻译领域里的知名教授或专家，有国外留学经历，且具有扎实的英汉双语语言功底，曾翻译出版多部译著和翻译作品，并且主持和参与过多项翻译项目的研究。我阅读李昌银教授发来的文库翻译人员名单，发现多名我所熟悉的知名教授、博士也在其中，感到格外放心。

“云南少数民族经典作品英译文库”的出版发行是云南省翻译界的一件大事，也是我国少数民族典籍翻译传来的又一佳音。想当年，我和“大中华文库”总协调人李林老师曾在参加全国典籍英译学术研讨会之余一起找到李昌银教授，敦促李教授向学校和同事呼吁，少数民族典籍翻译及研究是富矿，值得快挖、深挖，能早出成果，出大成果。今天，我们当年的心愿变成了美好的现实，心里感到特别高兴。再次热烈祝贺“云南少数民族经典作品英译文库”的顺利出版！

（王宏，中国典籍翻译研究会副会长、苏州大学博士生导师）

Foreword by Wang Hong

My friend Professor Li Changyin of Yunnan Normal University asked me to write a few words for the publication of *Classics of Yunnan Ethnic Groups in English Translation*. I am more than delighted to do it. As I have been doing research in English translation of Chinese classics, I know how important this work is. In recent years, substantial progress has been made in translating Chinese ethnic classics into English and introducing them to the world. Let's look at the following accomplishments.

First of all, several projects in the English translation of ethnic classics have received funding from the National Planning Office of Philosophy and Social Science. The first of these projects is *The Epic of Baeuqloxgdoh* (Zhuang-Chinese-English trilingual version), given funding in 2008 and headed by Professor Han Jiaquan of Baise University in Guangxi Zhuang Autonomous Region. In December 2013, this translation won the Shanhua Award, the most prestigious prize for folk literature and art in China. The second project is *A Study of the Manchu Archives*, written by Professor Wu Songlin of Northeastern University at Qinhuangdao and which was given funding in 2014. The third is *English*

Translation and Study of the Major Classics of the Tujia Ethnic Group, headed by Professor Zhang Liyu of the South-Central University for Nationalities, also granted in 2014.

Secondly, several English translations have been published. In 2012, *Liao Songs of Pingguo Zhuang*, has been listed as one of China's national intangible cultural heritages. It was translated by the School of Foreign Languages, Baise University, and published by Guangxi Normal University Press. Also in 2012, *Jangar* (a Chinese-English bilingual edition), edited by Professor Wu Songlin of Northeastern University at Qinhuangdao, was published by Jilin University Press. In 2013, *Tibetan Gnomic Verses Translated into English*, translated by Professor Li Zhengshuan of Hebei Normal University, was published by Changchun Press. And in 2014, *Heroic Geser Khan*, translated by Professor Wu Songlin of Northeastern University at Qinhuangdao, was published by Jilin University Press.

And thirdly, two important monographs have been published by The Ethnic Publishing House in the *Ethnic Classics Translation Research Series* edited by Professor Wang Hongyin of Nankai University. One is *A Study on the English Translation of* Ashima *by Gladys Taylor* (2013), which was the PhD dissertation of Professor Cui Xiaoxia of Yunnan University of Finance and Economics. The other is *Translation and Dissemination of the Oral Epic Manas* (2015) written by Associate Professor Liang Zhenhui of Xi'an International

Studies University.

Meanwhile, it is encouraging to see that the first conferences on English translation of ethnic classics in China have been held in Guangxi Nationalities University and Dalian Nationalities Institute respectively. Participants were both many and enthusiastic. Many papers were presented and a lot of topics discussed. The third conference will be hosted by South Central Nationalities University in 2016.

Why, then, has this field attracted so much attention from translators and scholars alike and accomplished so much in just a few years? The answer, I believe, lies in a rethinking of what constitutes Chinese classics as an indispensable part of human heritage. We used to see Chinese classics as more or less equal to the classics of the Han people, excluding works by other ethnic groups. Moreover, when we talk about Chinese classics, we focus too much on the literary works of ancient times. Yet Chinese classics actually refer to "important works and books before 1911, the year when the Qing dynasty fell, bringing an end to imperial rule". This definition requires us to pay attention not just to literary works, but also writings in other subjects, such as philosophy, science, law, medicine, economics, military affairs, astronomy, and geography, not only Han works, but writings by other ethnic groups as well.

The classical works of a nation are its archetypal symbols, the major carriers of its cultural genes. Chinese classics make up the core of Chinese tradition. The Chinese nation consists of 56 ethnic groups. Ethnic classics are an important part of not only Chinese traditional culture, but also world civilization. The translation of these works into other languages is important in that it helps to promote cross-cultural communications between China and other countries and to protect and preserve the uniqueness and diversity of ethnic cultures by making them accessible to foreign readers.

Chinese ethnic classics cover a variety of areas, such as religion, literature, history, language, medicine, astrology, and calendar, with numerous editions, special media and unique ways of transmission from generation to generation. Take, for example, *An Anthology of Chinese Ethnic Classics*, a colossal project that includes 110 volumes, 20 of which, from 23 ethnic groups, have been published. The anthology reflects the variety and quantity of China's ethnic classics and provides valuable material and resources for studying, understanding and developing Chinese culture and history in a more comprehensive and sustainable way.

The translation of Chinese ethnic classics into foreign languages is a very demanding job, involving rendering from ethnic languages to Chinese, between ethnic languages, and from ethnic languages (often via Chinese) to foreign languages. The first two types of translation can be traced back to the Spring and Autumn Period, when *The Song of the Yue People* was translated from their mother tongue into Chinese. The earliest translation of ethnic classics into a foreign language is *Wisdom of Royal Glory*, a long poem of the Uygurs, which was rendered from the source language into Arabic and is now in the Oriental Institute of Uzbekistan at Namangan. But it was not until modern times that the translation of ethnic classics into foreign languages accelerated. Noticeably, ethnic epics, such as *The Story of Prince Geser* of the Tibetans, *The Story of Jianggeer* of the Mongolians, *Manas* of the Kyrgyz, and narrative poems such as *Ashima* of the Yi people, *Alip and Salam* of the Uygurs, etc., have been published. These translations have contributed to acquainting the world with Chinese ethnic classics, but many remain to be translated.

Yunnan is rich in ethnic classics, boasting more than 100,000 volumes of written classics and over 40,000 pieces of oral literature. Relying on such bountiful resources, as a collective endeavor of the translation team of the School of Foreign Languages and Literature, Yunnan Normal University and with the help of Yunnan People's Publishing House, *Classics of Yunnan Ethnic Groups in English Translation* is the first project to translate Yunnan ethnic classics into English on a large scale. The School adheres to a professional spirit and academic standard in carrying out the project by selecting the most authoritative texts in the source language (Chinese) and recruiting the best translators from its huge faculty. The selection of the works, covering eleven of the twenty-five ethnic groups of the province, indicates expertise and insight. The implementation of the project will change the embarrassing obscurity of Yunnan ethnic classics by making them known to the world, many of them for the first time.

In light of disciplinary development, the project is of great importance, too. Participating in the translation will strengthen the academic foundation of the teachers, enrich their experience and enhance their translation skills and research ability. This in turn will help them become better teachers and thus able to educate students with higher quality. The publication of the books will add greatly to the faculty accomplishments of the School and raise the academic standing of Yunnan Normal University by taking the first step in this direction among the universities of Yunnan province.

This publication project is a great event not only for Yunnan itself, but also for China. Looking back, I remember that Professor Li Changyin, our friend Li Lin, editor of the *Library of Chinese Classics*, and I talked enthusiastically about initiating something like this in Yunnan when we attended a conference on the translation of ethnic classics in Soochow. Lin and I strongly suggested that Professor Li do it as soon as possible. Now I am very pleased to see our talk becoming reality. Again, my congratulations on the publication of *Classics of Yunnan Ethnic Groups in English Translation*!

(Wang Hong, Vice Chairman of Classics Translation Committee of CACSEC, PhD supervisor at Soochow University)

导 言

“云南少数民族经典作品英译文库”旨在将云南少数民族的经典作品翻译介绍给国外对其感兴趣的英文读者大众。随着以古代汉文经典构成的“大中华文库”的出版发行，学界正将注意力转移到民族典籍的翻译上来。民族典籍是指由民族作家创作的反应民族历史和文化的经典作品。广西、贵州、辽宁、新疆、西藏等省区的大学已经捷足先登。我们云南也理应有所作为。云南拥有全国最多的少数民族。全省25个少数民族中，有15个为云南特有民族，即阿昌族、白族、布朗族、傣族、德昂族、独龙族、哈尼族、景颇族、基诺族、拉祜族、傈僳族、纳西族、怒族、普米族、佤族。这些民族的典籍，有的是原作，有的是汉译本，构成了一个巨大的宝库，我们有义务将其介绍给国外的英语读者和学术界。问题是，先译什么？

云南所有的25个少数民族都创造了自己的经典作品，包括史诗、神话、创世故事、民谣、戏曲、山歌和丧歌，以各种形式流传于各地，总数不下10万卷，这还不包括口传文体。经过调查研究，并征求民族学专家的建议后，我们决定重点翻译史诗和神话。史诗和神话叙述的是民族起源故事，最能反映各民族哲学、历史、文化等的概貌、渊源。我们从汗牛充栋的民族史诗与神话中精选了云南阿昌族、白族、傣族、德昂族、哈尼族、景颇族、拉祜族、苗族、纳西族、普米族、彝族等 11 个少数民族的 17 部最具有代表性的经典作品。这些作品全部都是汉语译本，由既会讲母语又精通汉语的双语学者整理、翻译而成。其中有的是在节庆仪式和表演时从口语录制而来。我们没有选择用民族语言写成的文本，首先是因为很难寻找到民族语和英语俱佳的译者；其次是因为一部分典籍的民族语言文本在民间以多种方言形式流传，情节五花八门。汉语文本系专家仔细整理、翻译而成，因而更具权威性。接下来的问题是：如何译?

在我们选定的 17 部作品中，除了《白国因由》为散文体之外，其余全部为民歌韵文体，诗行长度大致相当，行末有松散押韵，无格律。译诗为诗是最起码的要求。我们遵循的原则有如下几点。

一、若原文为诗歌，译文也必须为诗歌。

二、译文尽可能完整地再现原文的思想内容和意象。

三、译文尽可能再现原文的修辞手段。

四、不改变原文每一节诗的行数，除非万不得已。

五、不使用英文的标准格律，因为原文并不是标准的格律体。采用英文的自然节奏，但诗行长短应大体一致。

六、不用韵，除非符合英文表达习惯且不损害原文内容。

我们所追求的，用苏珊·巴斯奈特的话来说就是“异地播种”，而不是直接移栽树木。关于原文的形式特征，尤其是尾韵，能再现时再现，不能再现时果断放弃。

那谁来翻译呢？本文库是云南师范大学外国语学院的集体项目，因此我们的翻译团队由本院十几位同行加上两位在职攻读翻译专业硕士学位的高校教师组成。所有译者都在高校教授翻译课程，从事翻译研究，不仅发表了翻译论文，也出版了译著。

传统上，人们通常是将外语译为母语，而不是将母语译为外语。但是这种情况正在发生改变。现在许多译者都将母语译为外语。根据耐克·帕科恩[①]和斯图亚特·坎贝尔[②]的论证，将母语译入非母语，能够达到相当高的水平。中国的情形为他们的观点提供了新的论据。中国典籍英译在19世纪由英国汉学家理雅各和翟理斯发起，20世纪在亚瑟·伟利、戴维·霍克思、波顿·沃森、约翰·闵福德、宇文所安等英美汉学家的推动下继续发展。值得注意的是，在这一过程中，旅居西方的华人学者迅速加入到了中国典籍英译的行列中。其中最著名的是辜鸿铭和林语堂。他们主动承担这个任务，因为他们认为西方汉学家的母语并非汉语，其译文往往误读汉语原文本，误解中国文化，自己义不容辞，必须为英语读者提供更忠实的英文翻译。自20世纪50年代开始，越来越多的中国大陆译者投身于典籍英译或重译。在杨宪益、许渊冲、汪榕培、王宏印、王宏、李正栓等当代翻译家和翻译理论家的积极倡导和引领下，典籍英译蔚然成风，势头强劲。许渊冲、王宏、李正栓等都在西方出版社出版了英文译著，这表明他们的英文水平达到了国际上的出版标准。

就本文库而言，我们采取了一系列保障译文质量的措施。我们要求译者尽最大努力拿出代表自己最高水平的译文。文

① 挑战公理：译入非母语. 阿姆斯特丹：约翰·本杰明斯出版公司，2005.
② 译入第二语言. 纽约：劳特里奇出版社，2013.

库的主编们对译文进行仔细研读，纠正理解偏差、语法错误以及格式上的问题。在此基础上，我们采取了一个不可或缺的步骤，请长期在我院从事英语教学工作的美国老师包琼（Joan Cecile Boulerice）对每一个译本进行逐字逐句的修改，使之更自然流畅，更符合英文表达习惯。我们尽了最大的努力。如果译文还存在什么问题，皆由我们负责，与包琼老师无关。

在这里，我们对所有给予我们宝贵帮助和支持的专家学者深表谢忱。感谢云南人民出版社的领导为文库成功申报为“十三五”国家重点出版物出版规划项目和国家出版基金项目给予的大力支持。感谢文库责编、东南亚南亚读物编辑部主任郭木玉，她的严谨和敬业令我们动容。感谢云南师范大学为文库提供了出版资金支持，使译者们不被“眼前的苟且”干扰，能够一心一意地追求“诗和远方”。感谢李正栓教授和王宏教授不仅一直鼓励我们前进，而且欣然为文库作序，从全球视野对其意义进行肯定，极大地提振了我们的信心。感谢包琼老师，她的修改保证了译文的流畅性。最后要特别感谢王宏教授和湖南人民出版社的资深编辑李林先生，是他们的建议促成了本文库的构想。

云南师范大学外国语学院

“云南少数民族经典作品英译文库”编委会

General Introduction

This publication project, *Classics of Yunnan Ethnic Groups in English Translation*, aims at introducing Yunnan ethnic classical works to the world by making them available to native speakers of English who might be interested in them. With the publication of the *Library of Chinese Classics*, which consists only of books written by Han authors in classical Chinese, attention now is being turned to the English translation and publication of ethnic classics, books produced by ethnic writers about their history and culture. Universities in provinces such as Guangxi, Guizhou, Liaoning, Xinjiang, and Xizang, have taken the initiative. We in Yunnan must do something, because Yunnan has the largest number of ethnic groups in China. 15 of the 25 ethnic groups in the province, the Achang, the Bai, the Bulang, the Dai, the De'ang, the Dulong, the Hani, the Jingpo, the Jinuo, the Lahu, the Lisu, the Naxi, the Nu, the Pumi, and the Wa, live in no other place but Yunnan. The classics of these people, either in their own language or in Chinese translations, are a great treasure house, which should be accessible to English readers and scholars. But what works should be translated first?

All the 25 ethnic groups in Yunnan have their classics,

epics, mythology, creation stories, folksongs, folk drama, mountain songs, and funeral lament lyrics, most of which exist in different versions in different places. According to one estimation, there are more than 100,000 volumes of them, excluding those in oral form. After a thorough survey and extensive consultations with experts of ethnic studies, we concluded that priority must be given to epics and mythologies, as they reflect an ethnic people's philosophy, history and culture more than anything else by narrating the stories of where and how they think they came from. From many epics and mythologies, we selected 17 of the most authoritative and popular classics representing 11 Yunnan ethnic groups, the Achang, the Bai, the Dai, the De'ang, the Hani, the Jingpo, the Lahu, the Miao, the Naxi, the Pumi, and the Yi. These works are all in Chinese, translated from the original by bilingual scholars whose mother tongue is their own ethnic language and who are fluent and proficient in Chinese. Some were recorded from their oral form at rituals and performances. We did not choose texts written in the ethnic language, not least because it is very hard to find a translator who is skilled in both the ethnic language and English. Moreover, some of the classics in the ethnic language were circulated in various oral forms and fragments. The published Chinese versions have been carefully edited and translated, hence they are more reliable. The next question is: how to translate them?

It happens that all of the 17 works except one are in verse form, with lines more or less the same length and loose rhymes, but no regular meter. A poem must be rendered into a poem; anything less is unacceptable. So here are the general rules we follow when doing the translation.

One. If the original is verse, the translated text must be verse, too.

Two. Reproduce the ideas and the images of the original as completely as possible.

Three. Reproduce the figures of speech of the original as much as possible.

Four. Do not change the number of lines in a stanza unless absolutely necessary.

Five. Do not use standard meters in English, because the Chinese original does not follow any regular meter. Use the natural rhythm of English instead, but most of the lines should look more or less the same length.

Six. Do not use rhyme unless it comes naturally and is faithful to the content of the original.

What we try to do is, to use Susan Bassnett's words, "transplant the seed", not the tree itself. As for the various aspects of form, particularly meter and end rhyme, we reproduce them when it is possible and abandon them when it is necessary.

Who will do the translations? As this is a collective project of the School of Foreign Languages and Literature of Yunnan Normal University, our team consists of a dozen faculty members and two students from our MA translation program who are already teachers in other universities. All the translators have been teaching translation and doing translation research for a long time. They have published not just academic articles on translation, but also translated books from English to Chinese or vice versa.

Traditionally, people translate into their mother tongue, not into a foreign language. But the situation is changing. Many translators today are translating from their mother tongue into a foreign language. The quality can be good, as Nike K. Pokorn and Stuart Campbell prove in *Challenging the Traditional Axioms: Translation into a non-mother tongue* (Amsterdam: John Benjamins Publishing Company, 2005) and *Translation into the Second Language* (New York: Routledge, 2013) respectively. The case of China provides further evidence for their argument. The translation of Chinese classics into English was initiated by James Legge and Herbert Allen Giles in the 19th century and carried on in the 20th century by Arthur Waley, David Hawkes, Burton Watson, John Minford, Stephen Owen and others. It is noticeable that these English and American sinologists were soon joined by Chinese scholars residing in the West, such as Hongming (Tomson) Gu and Lin Yutang, among others. They took up the job because they thought it was their obligation to give English readers more faithful translations than Western sinologists could, who, as their target language is their mother tongue, often misinterpret the original text and misrepresent Chinese culture. Since the 1950s, there has been an increasingly powerful trend for Mainland Chinese translators to render or re-render Chinese classics into foreign languages, English in particular. In our time, this work is gathering momentum, enthusiastically advocated and actively practiced by such well-known translation experts as Yang Xianyi of Beijing Foreign Language Press, Xu Yuanchong of Beijing University, Wang Rongpei of Dalian Foreign Language Institute, Wang Hongyin of Nankai University, Wang Hong of Soochow University, Li Zhengshuan of Hebei Normal University, and many more. These professors are not just translators, but also scholars in translation studies. More importantly, some of them, Xu Yuanchong, Wang Hong and Li Zhengshuan, for example, have had their translations published by Western publishers, which suggests that their English meets the international standard.

In the case of our project, we request that the translators do their best to produce good translations. When they submit them to us, they should represent the highest level that they can attain. Then the general editors appointed by the School read the translated texts and remove inaccurate renderings and grammar mistakes if there are any. On top of that, we've taken an indispensable measure to ensure that our English is readable. We asked Ms. Joan Cecile Boulerice, an American teacher who has been teaching English in our school since 2009, to read every text that we've translated and improve the English by making it more natural and idiomatic. This is the best we can do. Of course any problems that still remain in the translations are ours. They have nothing to do with our American teacher.

As the project is well under way, we would like to thank all those who have helped to make it possible. Ms. Guo Muyu, director of the South and Southeast Asia Editorial Department, Yunnan People's Publishing House, has been most helpful in our cooperation. In addition, she has added importance to the project by turning it into a national publication project. Yunnan Normal University has supported us by paying the publication fees so that the translators won't have to be burdened with the financial responsibilities for this project. Professor Li Zhengshuan and Professor Wang Hong not only have always encouraged us to go on but have also written the forewords for the project, putting it in a global perspective. Ms. Joan Cecile Boulerice's revision has ensured the fluency of the translated texts. Finally, special thanks must be given to Professor Wang Hong, again, and Mr. Li Lin of Hunan People's Press for their suggestion that has helped us conceive the project from the very beginning.

The General Editors
School of Foreign Languages & Literature
Yunnan Normal University, Kunming

牡帕密帕

目录

目录

Mupamipa

Contents

Mupamipa

Contents

歌头
Prologue

兄弟姐妹们，

听吧，

响篾吹得多么清脆，

芦笙吹得多么悠扬；

看吧，

舞步那么坚强有力，

姿态那么爽朗豪放。

我们和睦地坐在一起，

紧紧围着温暖的火塘。

我们唱支古老的山歌，

欢欢畅畅玩一场。

颂扬祖先的业绩，

祝愿我们未来的美好时光。

Brothers and sisters,
Oh listen!
The jaw harp is so melodious,
The lusheng[1] is so mellifluous.
Oh behold!
We dance so vigorously,
We move so sprightly.
In harmony we sit together,
Around the cozy fire.
Singing an ancient mountain song,
We are happy and merry.
We praise our ancestors' deeds,
We pray for good days to come.

① Lusheng is a local ethnic musical instrument.

第一章　造天造地

Canto 1　Creation of the Sky and the Earth

在很久很久以前，
没有地也没有天，
没有风和雨，
日月星辰都不见。

白天黑夜分不清，
东南西北无法辨，
迷雾茫茫的日子呵，
不知过了多少年。

宇宙在沉睡，
独有厄莎天神未合眼；
宇宙好像蜘蛛网，
厄莎坐在网中间。

厄莎苦思苦想，
天天坐卧不安。
厄莎睡着想，
睡破了九床垫子；
厄莎站着想，
踩坏了九双鞋子。

Long, long ago,
There was no earth nor sky,
Nor wind nor rain,
Nor stars, nor sun, nor moon.

Day was not separated from night.
The Four Directions were not discernible.
The world was a foggy void
For nobody knows how many years.

The universe was fast asleep.
Only God Esha was wide awake,
Sitting at the center of the cosmos,
Which was like a spider web.

He thought and thought,
Worried every day.
He thought while sleeping,
Wearing out nine mattresses.
He thought while standing,
Wearing out nine pairs of shoes.

厄莎急出三身大汗，
进进出出打转转。

厄莎搓下脚手汗，
做了四棵柱子：
金柱子，
银柱子，
铜柱子，
铁柱子。
又做了四条大鱼：
大金鱼，
大银鱼，
大铜鱼，
大铁鱼。
柱子明晃晃，
大鱼光灿灿。

柱子支在鱼背上，
再架四棵天梁，
再架四棵地梁，
天椽放在天梁上，
地椽放在地梁上，
从此天地分开了，

He sweated buckets three times,
Rushing in and out anxiously.

Rubbing the dirt off his hands and feet,
He turned it into four pillars:
A gold pillar,
A silver pillar,
A copper pillar,
And an iron pillar.
He made four giant fish, too:
A gold fish,
A silver fish,
A copper fish,
And an iron fish.
The pillars were brilliant.
The fish were bright.

The pillars were placed on the fish's back,
Four sky beams were put up,
Four earth beams were put up.
The sky rafters were placed on the sky beams,
The earth rafters were fixed on the earth beams.
Now the sky and the earth were separated,

厄莎心里好喜欢。

厄莎搓下脚手汗，
揉成很多很多泥巴团。
七万七千个做天网，
七万七千个做地网，
从此天像个罩子，
地像一块木板。

天做成了，
地做成了，
可是，天没骨头是软的，
地没骨头要下陷。

厄莎又辗转思索，
不知想了多少时间。
他忍痛抽出自己身上的骨头。
手骨架在天上成天骨，
脚骨架在地上成地骨，
天有天骨硬铮铮，
地有地骨不下陷。

天有多高啊？

Esha's heart filled with pleasure.

He then rubbed more dirt off his hands and feet,
And rolled it into many, many balls,
Turning seventy-seven thousand into a sky web,
And another seventy-seven thousand into an earth web.
Since then, the sky has been like a canopy,
And the earth resembles a wooden board.

The sky and the earth were created,
But, without bones,
The sky would be loose,
And the earth would sink.

Esha thought hard
For nobody knows how long.
Then he removed some bones from his body,
Using his arm bones as the sky's bones
And his leg bones as the earth's bones.
With bones, the sky became solid.
With bones, the earth would not sink.

How high was the sky?

地有多厚啊？
厄莎不放心，
派了两只穿山甲去查看。

一只钻到天上，
一只钻到地下，
它们回来对厄莎讲：
天地厚薄都一样，
就是天小了，地大了，
地和天合拢，
天要撑大，
地要收缩。

厄莎皱着眉头想，
心翻波澜不安详。
造天的助手是扎罗，
造地的助手是娜罗，
娜罗仔细又勤快，
扎罗粗犷又懒惰。
天小了，
地大了，
厄莎又重新把天撑大，
将地收缩。

How thick was the earth?
Esha was so worried that
He sent two pangolins over to have a look.

One of them went into the sky,
And the other dug into the earth.
They told him when they came back:
The earth was as thick as the sky was high,
But the sky was too small, the earth was too big.
If they were to fit each other,
The sky must be widened,
And the earth must be reduced.

Esha knitted his brows,
Racking his brains for a solution.
Zhaluo was his assistant in creating the sky,
Naluo was his assistant in creating the earth.
Naluo was careful and diligent,
But Zhaluo was careless and lazy.
As the sky was too small,
And the earth was too big,
Esha had to enlarge the one
And shrink the other.

天撑大了，
像一口闪亮的铁锅；
地缩小了，
凸凹不平，
像那数不清的田螺。

天造好了，
地造好了，
厄莎住在北京，
北京就在地中央。
北京有九间房子，
北京有九十九座高山。
幢幢房子高又高，
山头峰岭插云霄。

天有了，
地有了，
可是没有太阳，
可是没有月亮，
可是没有星星。
没有日月星辰，
万物不会生长。

The enlarged sky looked
Like a shining iron pot.
The shrunken earth was uneven,
As if it were covered with
Numerous river snails.

The sky was completed,
And the earth was perfected.
Esha resided in Beijing,
Right in the center of the earth.
In Beijing there were nine houses.
In Beijing there were ninety-nine mountains.
The houses were extremely high,
And the peaks touched the sky.

Now there was the sky,
Now there was the earth,
But there was no sun,
Nor moon,
Nor stars.
Without them,
Things would not grow.

厄莎用左眼做太阳，
厄莎用右眼做月亮。
可是太阳不会发热，
月亮不会放光。
厄莎去问太阳，
厄莎去问月亮：
“你为什么不发热？
你为什么不放光？”
他们回答厄莎：
“温暖和光明，
潜藏在我们身上，
万物都要降临，
如果没有武器自卫，
怕敌人将我们损伤。”

太阳上的斑点，
是豹子咬的伤痕；
月亮脸上的那块黑影，
是青蛙的爪子把她踏脏。
太阳偎着厄莎，
月亮蹲在地上，
聆听厄莎的吩咐，

Esha made a sun with his left eye
And a moon with his right eye.
But the sun would not produce heat,
And the moon would not give off light.
So he went to ask the sun
And the moon:
"Why don't you produce heat?
Why don't you give off light?"
In reply, they told him:
"Warmth and light
Are hidden in our bodies.
But, as all things will come to the world,
We must have weapons to protect ourselves
From bad creatures before giving off warmth and light."

Indeed, the black spots on the sun
Were scars left by the leopard's teeth,
And the shadow on the moon
Was the frog's paw print.
The sun snuggled up to Esha,
While the moon squatted on the ground,
Listening to his instructions,

等候厄莎的主张。

厄莎没有吃饭，
厄莎没有喝水，
厄莎踱着沉重的步子，
专心致意，沉思苦想。
厄莎拔下头发当银针，
厄莎呵出口气当金针，
银针插在月亮头上，
金针插在太阳头上。

金针硬铮铮，
刺眼又发烫；
银针很柔软，
发光又冰凉。

豹子怕烫躲在林子里，
青蛙怕冷便往水底藏。
太阳展开了金色翅膀——
万里腾空，气势磅礴；
月亮架起皎洁的轮盘，
在天际中运转飞翔。

Awaiting his suggestions.

Esha didn't eat
Or drink anything.
He paced back and forth
In a pensive mood.
He created silver needles with his hair.
He made gold needles by breathing out some air.
He planted the silver needles on the moon.
He stuck the gold needles on the sun.

The gold needles were hard,
Glaring and hot.
The silver needles were soft,
Shiny and cool.

Leopards hid in the wood to avoid the heat.
Frogs stayed under water to keep warm.
The sun spread its golden wings,
Taking off brilliantly and majestically.
The moon rode on a white disk,
Moving across the heavens.

太阳转呵，
月亮飞呵，
忙坏了月亮，
累坏了太阳。

厄莎告诉月亮：
十二天是一轮；
厄莎告诉太阳：
十二个月是一年。
雄鸡喔喔太阳升，
谷雀喳喳太阳落。
太阳白天东山起，
月亮夜间照地上。

太阳暴晒染红了白鹇的脚，
月亮生露润花了白鹇的羽毛。
厄莎的手茧变成了白云，
厄莎的汗珠变成了星星。
朝霞是天空的花环，
薄雾是大地的头巾。

呵，天宇多美丽，
呵，地面多宽广。

The sun ran and ran,
Until it was exhausted.
The moon flew on and on
Until it was fatigued.

Esha told the moon:
Twelve days constitute one round.
He also told the sun:
Twelve months made up one year.
The sun rose when the rooster crowed
And set when the sparrows chirped.
The sun rose in the east at daybreak.
The moon illuminated the earth at night.

The sun's heat dyed the silver pheasant's feet red.
The moon's dew made its feathers colorful.
The calluses of Esha's palm became white clouds.
His sweat drops turned into stars.
The rosy dawn was the sky's garland.
The thin mist was the earth's shawl.

Oh, how beautiful the sky was!
Oh, how vast the earth was!

厄莎搓着脚汗，

厄莎搓着手汗，

他筹划着新的主意，

瞭望着无边无际的远方。

Esha rubbed the dirt
Off his feet and hands,
Conceiving something new,
Looking into the distance.

第二章 造物造人

Canto 2 Creation of Nature and Human Beings

白鹇天上飞三遍，
白鹇地下飞三转，
天边地角都看过，
一滴水珠也不见。

大地红彤彤，
烈日像火焰。
白鹇找不到水喝，
咿咿呀呀直叫唤。

厄莎搓下脚手汗，
两只鸭子就出现。
厄莎给它们一对银翅膀，
厄莎给它们一对金脚板。

鸭子天上飞三遍，
鸭子地下飞三转。
它们回到厄莎面前，
一齐把求水的办法贡献：
山上挖塘，
山脚开沟，

Three times the silver pheasant flew across the sky.
Three times it flew around the earth.
It searched every corner of the world,
But found not one drop of water.

The hot sun sent out flames.
The earth was burning.
The thirsty silver pheasant
Cried miserably.

Esha rubbed the dirt off his feet and hands.
It turned into two ducks.
He gave them silver wings.
He gave them golden feet.

Three times the ducks flew across the sky.
Three times they flew around the earth.
When they came back to Esha,
They told him how to get water:
Water would appear
If ponds were made on the mountains,

多种芭蕉林，
水就会出现。

厄莎领着扎罗和娜罗，
挖了九天塘子，
开了九天大沟，
挖了塘子七十七拿深，
开了大沟七十七拿长 。[1]
鹌鹑打开厄莎的箱子，
送来箱子里装着的种子。
白鹇撒种子，
鸭子撒种子，
种子撒了七十七条沟，
种子撒了七十七座山。

芭蕉种下三天，
厄莎天天去查看，
一天去三趟，
每趟出大汗。

芭蕉种下三轮，

① 拿：古时民间衡量长度的方法，一拿约5市尺。这里的七十七拿不是实际深度和长度，意为很深、很长。

Ditches were dug at the foot of the mountains,
And more banana seeds were sown.

With the help of Zhaluo and Naluo,
Esha spent nine days making ponds
As deep as seventy-seven arm-span lengths.①
He spent another nine days digging ditches
As long as seventy-seven arm-span lengths.
Quails opened Esha's box
And took out the seeds.
The silver pheasant scattered the seeds
In seventy-seven ditches.
The ducks scattered the seeds
Over seventy-seven mountains.

Three days after the banana seeds were sown,
Esha went to have a look.
He went three times a day,
Sweating heavily each time.

Banana seeds had been sown three rounds,

① Arm span is a unit of measurement equalling about 1.67 metres. Seventy-seven arm-span lengths is not a real number here. It suggests that the ponds are very deep and the ditches are very long.

种子还不发芽，
厄莎每天去三趟，
每趟出大汗。

大汗流满了塘子，
大汗流满了大沟，
大汗滋润着种子，
大汗抚育出了芽子。

厄莎用金子做芭蕉根，
厄莎用绸缎做芭蕉心。
根子深深扎地下，
芭蕉叶子翠生生。

鸭子住在水塘里，
鹌鹑守着芭蕉林。
水波银晃晃，
芭蕉绿茵茵。
它们高高兴兴，
赞颂厄莎的智慧和聪明。

天气晴又明，
野草绿如茵，

But they wouldn't germinate.
Esha went to check three times a day,
Sweating all over each time.

His sweat filled up
The ponds and ditches,
Nourishing the seeds,
Which soon sprouted.

Esha made banana roots with gold,
Which pierced deeply into the soil.
He turned satin into the cores of banana trees,
So that the banana leaves grew verdant.

The ducks lived in the ponds,
Where the water was crystal clear.
The quails protected the banana trees,
Which were lush green.
Happily, they sang praise for
Esha's ingenuity and wisdom.

The weather was sunny.
The grass was luxuriant.

就在这时节，
厄莎种下一棵树。

时间过了三轮，
苗儿长高了，
但不发桠，不分枝，
没叶没花光秃秃的一身。

厄莎告诉扎罗和娜罗，
要他们站在树下培育树苗。
扎罗走在树下伸开手，
树苗分枝了；
娜罗走在树下指着包头，
树苗发叶了；
娜罗指着耳环，
树苗开花了。
从此，树木穿上盛装——
枝叶密茂，花儿鲜艳。

花儿开了，
果子结了，
没有炎热，
没有寒冷，

It was at this time
That Esha planted a tree.

Three rounds passed,
The seedling grew up,
But it did not branch out
Or have leaves or flowers.

Esha told Zhaluo and Naluo
To cultivate seedlings under the tree.
Zhaluo spread out his hands
And the tree branched out.
Naluo pointed at her head-wrapper
And the tree began to have leaves.
She then pointed at her earring
And the tree blossomed.
Since then, trees have dressed themselves up
With luxuriant leaves and colorful flowers.

Flowers were in bloom,
Trees bore fruit,
But the fruit could not ripen
Or taste sweet,

果子不会熟，
味道不会甜。

扎罗看手骨，
娜罗看脚骨，
手脚骨头十二节。
冷季三个月，
热季九个月，
一年定为十二个月。

花儿有开有谢，
果子落了又结，
果子甜又香呵，
厄莎心喜悦。
厄莎晒干了果子，
厄莎磨细了果子。
厄莎吹口气，
果沫飘空中，
花儿遍地开，
果子遍地结，
树木杂草遍地生，
百兽满山野，
百鸟齐飞跃。

Because there was
Neither heat nor cold.

Zhaluo counted his finger bones.
Naluo counted her toe bones.
The number was twelve for both.
Thus one year was stipulated as twelve months:
The cold season would be three months
And the hot season would be nine months.

Flowers bloomed and withered alternately.
The tree bore fruit once every year.
Esha was delighted,
The fruit was sweet and fragrant.
He dried the fruit in the sun
And ground it into powder,
Which he blew into the air.
Then suddenly,
Flowers bloomed everywhere,
There was fruit in every place,
Trees and grass grew all over the mountains,
All kinds of animals played on the land
And all kinds of birds flew in the sky.

扎罗、娜罗四处察看，
三天三夜不眠。
扎罗、娜罗回报厄莎：
“花儿开得繁盛。
只有泡竹、茨竹，
竹节瘦弱，
叶儿枯卷。”

厄莎听了这话，
立即叫把话传：
“茨竹调到平坝，
泡竹调到山垭。”
死了的茨竹发出了嫩叶，
干枯的泡竹冒出了笋尖。

扎罗、娜罗回报厄莎：
“飞鸟只能飞，
百兽只会走，
好像闷闷不乐，
默默无言。”

厄莎开挖出一条酒泉，

Zhaluo and Naluo inspected every place
For three days and nights, with no sleep.
They came back to report to Esha:
"All the flowers are in full bloom
Except the thin-walled bamboo and the thorny bamboo,
Whose tubes were weak
And whose leaves were sickly yellow."

Hearing this,
Esha gave orders:
"Move the thorny bamboo to flat land.
Transfer the thin-walled bamboo to the slopes."
Then the dying thorny bamboo had new leaves
And the dried thin-walled bamboo had tender shoots.

Zhaluo and Naluo reported to Esha:
"The birds can only fly.
The beasts can only walk about.
They both seem to be depressed,
Silent, with no words."

Esha dug a wine spring,

酒泉像小河流水潺潺，
泉水像花一样喷香，
像糖一样甜。

百兽喝了酒，
能说自己的话；
百鸟喝了酒，
唱起歌儿声婉转。

山中老鼠叫，
坝子小雀闹，
河里鱼儿在跳跃，
呵，就是人声听不到。
厄莎搭了一个窝棚，
用蕨菜做柱子，
用蒿子做横梁，
用茅草做篱笆，
一边靠着厄莎的房子，
一边靠着大石岩。

厄莎拣来火石，
用火链来打火。
三个火星飞起来，

Which bubbled on like a brook.
The wine was as fragrant as flowers
And as sweet as sugar.

The beasts drank the wine
And started to speak their own languages.
The birds drank the wine
And began to sing melodious songs.

In the mountains rats cried,
In the plains sparrows frolicked,
In the rivers fish jumped,
But no human voice was heard.
Esha set up a hut,
With brake ferns as pillars,
Wormwood as crossbeams,
Cogon grass as fences,
Connected to Esha's house on one side
And with a boulder on the other.

Esha found some flint
And struck it against an iron tool.
Three sparks flew up

火草燃着烧起来，
搓搓揉揉吹三下，
明晃晃的火焰冒出来。

厄莎打开一个箱子，
找出一颗葫芦籽，
把葫芦籽儿撒下地，
用草灰把籽种盖起来。

过了七轮又七天，
葫芦的藤子长出来，
素白色的花儿逗人爱。
叶子比簸箕还大，
又长又粗的藤子呵，
爬满了山箐伸到山梁外。

又过了七个月，
葫芦成熟了，
藤粗皮硬果子大，
扎罗、娜罗无法摘下来。

厄莎房后面，
果树几千万，

And the tinder was lit.
He rubbed it and blew three times
And red flames rose up.

Esha opened a box
And took out a gourd seed,
Which he sowed in the field,
Covering it with grass ashes.

After seven rounds and seven days,
A vine grew out of the gourd seed,
With a lovely white flower.
Its leaves were wider than a winnowing basket.
The vine was thick and long,
Crawling all over the valley, reaching beyond the ridge.

Seven months later,
The gourd grew up,
With a thick vine, hard skin and large fruit,
So large that Zhaluo and Naluo couldn't pick it up.

Behind Esha's house,
There were thousands of fruit trees,

果子颜色鲜，
味儿有酸又有甜。

麂子跳过去，
野牛走过来，
老熊走路慢吞吞，
猫头鹰站在树梢尖。

树上果子掉下来，
打在麂子鼻子上，
麂子受惊便乱跑，
吓得野牛踩断葫芦藤。

葫芦藤断了，
葫芦滚跑了。
滚到哪边山？
滚到哪条箐？

厄莎来查看，
葫芦早不见，
只有断藤一根，
枯萎的叶子掉在麂子脚边。

With bright-colored fruit,
Some sour, others sweet.

A muntjac leapt about,
A wild ox walked up,
A bear strolled slowly,
And an owl perched upon the tree top.

Some fruit dropped from the tree
And hit the muntjac on the nose,
Frightening the animal into a mad run,
Scaring the wild ox, who unfortunately broke the gourd vine.

When the vine was broken
The gourd rolled off.
Where did it go?
Which hill? Which vale?

Esha came for an inspection,
But the gourd was gone.
There was only a broken vine
And withered leaves beside the muntjac.

厄莎问麂子：
“葫芦藤子谁踩断？”
麂子说是野牛，
野牛说
是麂子乱跑吓破它的胆。
麂子眨眨眼，
没有再申辩。
但它责怪猫头鹰，
说它啄掉一串果子——
打中了它的脑门，
打伤了它的双眼。

厄莎很着急，
走回窝铺边，
寻来又寻去，
葫芦仍不见。
森林莽苍苍，
宿雾迷茫茫，
到哪条箐找葫芦？
到哪边山找葫芦？

厄莎追到芭蕉林，
芭蕉回答“没看见”，

He asked the muntjac:
“Who broke the gourd vine?”
The muntjac said it was the ox.
But the ox complained that
It was the muntjac who scared him.
The muntjac blinked his eyes
And made no more protest.
But he blamed the owl
For dropping some fruit,
Which hit him on the forehead
And hurt both his eyes.

Worried and disappointed,
Esha went back to his house,
Looking everywhere,
But found no gourd.
The wood was dark and deep,
The night mist hung over everything,
To which vale could he go to find the gourd?
And which hill?

Esha went to the banana forest,
But the bananas said they hadn’t seen it.

厄莎生气说：
“等到人出世，
让那串串果儿把你腰压弯。”

厄莎追到泡竹林，
泡竹回答“没看见”。
厄莎生气说：
“等到人出世，
砍下泡竹把墙壁编。”

厄莎追到茅草林，
茅草回答“没看见”。
厄莎生气说：
“等到人出世，
砍下茅草盖房子。”

厄莎追到金竹林，
金竹回答“没看见”。
厄莎生气说：
“等到人出世，
砍下金竹做响篾。”

厄莎追到松树林，

So he said angrily,
"When human beings are born,
You'll be bent low with strings of fruit."

Esha went to the thin-walled bamboo forest,
But the bamboos said they hadn't seen it.
So he said angrily,
"When human beings are born,
You'll be cut to weave house walls."

Esha went to the cogon grass bush,
But it said it hadn't seen the gourd.
So he said angrily,
"When human beings are born,
You'll be cut to thatch houses."

Esha went to the golden bamboo forest,
But the bamboos said they hadn't seen it.
So he said angrily,
"When human beings are born,
You'll be cut to make the jaw harp."

Esha went to the pine forest.

松树回答“看到了，
可是，双脚难移未追赶”。
厄莎听了很高兴，
送给松树红缎子：
“等到人出世，
把你砍来做明子。”

厄莎追到靛园中，
蓝靛回答“没看见”。
厄莎生气说：
“等到人出世，
用你把布染。”

跨过几条箐，
越过几座山，
厄莎的脸鼓胀得彤红，
厄莎的背流淌着冷汗。
厄莎不停步，
大步向前赶。

厄莎追到蒿树林，
蒿树回答“看见了，
只是无手未抓住”。

The pine trees answered,
"Yes, but we could not move our feet to catch it."
Esha was so happy that
He gave the pine trees some red satin, saying,
"When human beings are born,
You'll be cut to make resin."

Esha went to the indigo yard,
But the indigo said it hadn't seen the gourd.
So he said angrily,
"When human beings are born,
You'll be used to dye cloth."

Having crossed several valleys
And climbed over a few mountains,
Esha's face turned red,
And cold sweat ran down his back,
But he strode on in a hurry
Without stopping for one moment.

Esha went to the wormwood bush.
The wormwood said it had seen the gourd,
But, without hands, couldn't catch it.

厄莎听了很高兴：
“准你开花又结果，
等到人出世，
用你做甑子，
舂米做粑粑。”

厄莎追到茨竹林，
茨竹回答“没看见”。
厄莎生气说：
“将来人出世，
用你编篮、编箩、扭竹纤。”

厄莎追到黄栗树林，
黄栗树回答“没看见”。
厄莎生气说：
“等到人出世，
用你去做锄头、斧子把。”

厄莎到处问遍，
不知葫芦滚到哪边。
他沉思了半晌，
新的主意涌上心间。

Esha was happy to hear that, saying,
"You'll blossom and bear fruit.
When human beings are born,
You'll be woven into a rice steamer
To make rice cakes."

Esha went to the thorny bamboo forest,
But the thorny bamboos said they hadn't seen it.
So he said angrily,
"When human beings are born,
You'll be used to weave baskets and make ropes."

Esha went to the chestnut forest,
But the chestnut trees said they hadn't seen it.
So he said angrily,
"When human beings are born,
You'll be used as handles for plows and axes."

Esha went everywhere and asked everybody,
But still didn't know where the gourd had gone.
He thought and thought,
And hit upon an idea.

厄莎做了一对螃蟹，
两个夹，八只脚，
叫螃蟹到河里、海里寻找，
一定要找到葫芦他才心圆意满。

螃蟹钻进河里找，
螃蟹钻进海里找，
终于找到了葫芦。
螃蟹夹着葫芦上了岸，
葫芦的脖子夹细了，
葫芦喝多了海水，
葫芦的肚子胀得又大又圆。

葫芦夹上了岸，
厄莎把葫芦搬回了家，
葫芦放在晒台上。
葫芦喷出馥郁的香味，
日夜放射出耀眼的金光。

七十七天过去了，
葫芦晒干了，
葫芦里发出人的声音，
厄莎的心儿很激荡。

He made a pair of crabs,
With two big pincers and eight legs,
And sent them to the rivers and the sea.
He wouldn't be happy till they found the gourd.

The crabs went into
The rivers and the sea.
At last, they found the gourd
And came back to the shore with it.
Its neck had been made thin by their gripping.
The gourd drank so much seawater
That its belly swelled up like a ball.

Now the gourd was retrieved,
Esha carried it home
And placed it on his veranda,
Where it gave off an aroma
And a golden light day and night.

Seventy-seven days had passed
Before the gourd was dried.
Esha was excited to hear
Human voices coming out of it.

听吧！

葫芦里在唱：

“我们住在葫芦房，

从来没有见太阳。

哪个哥哥心肠好，

把我们接出葫芦房。

要是出了葫芦房，

苦出谷米他先尝。”

厄莎心喜欢，

忙得大汗淌，

叫来小米雀，

铁嘴就有九尺九寸长。

小米雀啄葫芦，

葫芦崩崩响，

好像敲起喜庆的鼓声，

迎接他们走出葫芦房。

小米雀啄一下，

嘴就啄痛了；

小米雀啄三下，

Oh listen!
There was singing in the gourd,
"We live in a gourd house.
We have never seen the sun.
Is there a brother out there kind enough
To help us get out of the gourd?
If we are out, you'll be the first
To taste the rice we grow."

Esha's heart filled with pleasure,
Even though he was sweating all over.
He asked the little sparrow
Whose iron beak was nine feet nine inches long for help.

The little sparrow pecked at the gourd,
Producing a bang-bang sound,
As if beating a ceremonial drum
To welcome them out of the gourd house.

The first peck
Made the sparrow's beak painful.
The first three pecks

嘴就啄秃了。
小米雀啄了三天三夜，
葫芦照旧硬梆梆。

厄莎叫来一对老鼠，
老鼠牙齿像铁锉。
它们日夜啃葫芦，
吱吱音响像祝贺：
葫芦人快点降临吧，
看看大地上多么欢乐。

老鼠啃了三天三夜，
葫芦壳出现两个洞，
葫芦人从洞里爬出来，
一男一女笑哈哈。

山在笑，
水在笑，
蓝天披彩霞，
万岭绣春花。

男的叫扎笛，
女的叫娜笛。

Made it blunt.
For three days and nights the sparrow pecked,
But the gourd was still safe and sound.

Esha called forth a pair of rats,
Whose teeth were as sharp as an iron file.
They gnawed at the gourd day and night,
Making squeaks that seemed to say,
Come out quick, Gourd Men,
And see how happy the world is!

The rats worked three days and nights,
Drilling two holes in the wall of the gourd.
Out crawled two laughing human beings,
A man and a woman.

The mountains laughed,
The rivers laughed,
The blue sky wore colorful clouds,
And the ridges were ornamented with flowers.

The boy was Zhadi.
Very stout was he.

扎笛很结实，

娜笛很秀气。

他们喝的是最甜的水，

他们吃的是最甜的蜜。

奖励小米雀吃谷子，

奖励老鼠吃白米。

老鼠、小米雀挺满意，

告别了扎笛和娜笛。

The girl was Nadi.
Quite slender was she.
They drank the sweetest water.
They ate the sweetest honey.
They rewarded the sparrows with millet
And thanked the rats with rice,
Which pleased them both,
So they said farewell to Zhadi and Nadi.

第三章 生活下去

Canto 3 Survival

一　扎笛、娜笛结婚

扎笛得到厄莎抚养，
长得结实健壮；
娜笛得到厄莎抚养，
长得白白胖胖。
扎笛像山上的红松，
娜笛像天上的月亮。

扎笛和娜笛，
渐渐长大了，
养一天等于十天，
长一年等于十年。

娜笛秉性温和、勤劳，
天天上山采菜拾菌。
扎笛心灵手巧，
天天做着石斧、竹刀。

扎笛砍来最好的泡竹做芦笙，
娜笛砍来最好的金竹做响篾；
弹起响篾像夜莺唱歌，

I. Zhadi and Nadi Getting Married

Cared for by Esha,
Zhadi was healthy and strong,
Like the red pines in the mountain.
Tended to by Esha,
Nadi was fair and plump,
Like the moon in the sky.

Zhadi and Nadi
Were growing up fast.
One day for them equaled ten for others.
One year for them meant ten for the rest.

Gentle and hard-working, Nadi picked vegetables
And mushrooms in the mountains every day.
Quick and deft, Zhadi never stopped making
Stone axes and bamboo knives in every way.

Zhadi cut the best thin-walled bamboo to make the lusheng.
Nadi cut the best golden bamboo to make the jaw harp.
The sound of the jaw harp was like the nightingale's song.

吹起芦笙像布谷鸟欢笑。

花儿谢了又开，
果子落了又结。
扎笛长大了，
娜笛长高了。

厄莎告诉扎笛、娜笛，
要他们同住一起，
像太阳月亮配成对，
像花木雀鸟形影不离。
扎笛、娜笛回答厄莎：
“我们同由一处来，
只能成为兄妹，
不能成为夫妻。”

扎笛跑到阿基山，
娜笛跑到阿约山，
山山相隔看不见，
扎笛、娜笛不想成夫妻。
厄莎神法大，
两座高山并一起。

The music of the lusheng was like the cuckoo's laughter.

Old flowers withered and new flowers bloomed.
Rotten fruit fell and small fruit grew.
Zhadi had grown into a young man,
And Nadi had become a tall lady.

Esha told Zhadi and Nadi
To live together, to be a couple
Like the sun and the moon,
Like flowers, trees and birds, united forever.
But Zhadi and Nadi replied,
"As we are from the same place,
We can only be brother and sister,
Not husband and wife."

Zhadi went to Aji Mountain.
Nadi went to Ayue Mountain.
Unwilling to become husband and wife,
They were separated by mountains.
But Esha brought the two mountains together
By his magic power.

扎笛跑到月亮里躲，
娜笛跑到太阳里藏。
厄莎做了两剂迷药，
包装在蜂儿身上。
蜂儿绕太阳一转，
蜂儿绕月亮一转。
扎笛闻到迷药回到地上，
娜笛闻到迷药回到扎笛身旁。

厄莎给响篾放上相思药，
厄莎给芦笙放上相思药；
扎笛吹芦笙就想到妹妹，
娜笛弹响篾就想到哥哥。

扎笛、娜笛当着厄莎害羞，
他们背地生活在一起；
他们成了夫妻，
从此他俩不再分离。

老鹰看见扎笛、娜笛结婚，
要去报告厄莎，
扎笛、娜笛央求说：
“不要告诉厄莎，

Zhadi fled to the moon,
And Nadi ran to the sun.
But Esha made two doses of magic potion
And tied it to the bee,
Which flew first around the sun
And then around the moon.
When Zhadi smelled it he returned to the earth.
When Nadi smelled it she came back to Zhadi.

Esha rubbed love potion
On the jaw harp and the lusheng.
Zhadi thought of his sister when he played the lusheng.
Nadi thought of her brother when she blew the jaw harp.

They felt shy in Esha's presence,
But they lived together secretly.
Being husband and wife,
They would never be separated.

When the eagle saw they were married,
It wanted to tell Esha.
But Zhadi and Nadi pleaded,
"Please don't tell him.

等我们有儿有女，
请你吃小鸡。”

二　第一代人

冬往春来，
一年已经过去。
娜笛脸儿红润，
但全身酸软无力。

她坐着站不起来，
她站着坐不下去，
吃喝不觉甜，
浑身上下不舒适。

娜笛跑到山箐里，
吃了三蓬酸藤，
吃完这些东西，
还是没有力气。

娜笛跑到山洞里，
看见几窝蜂蜜，
吃了这些东西，

When we have children,
We'll treat you to some chicks."

II. The First Generation of Humans

Winter was gone and spring was here.
One year had just passed.
Nadi's face turned red,
But she felt weak and tired.

She had difficulty getting up
And sitting down.
She had no taste for anything,
Feeling unwell all over.

Nadi went to the valley
And ate three clusters of sour vines.
But she still felt
Weak and tired.

Then she went to a cave
And found a lot of honey.
She ate it,

还是没有力气。

厄莎盘问娜笛：
“蜂蜜吃了九个山洞，
酸藤吃了九山九岭，
为什么没力气，
想必是身怀有孕？”
娜笛回答厄莎：
“只想吃酸的，
没有怀孩子。”

胎儿一天天长大，
婴儿快要下地。
可是全身无力，
娜笛去哪里寻找力气？

娜笛找到山沟里，
两手扶着枇杷树，
身子靠着枇杷树，
枇杷也能结果了。

娜笛找到坝子里，
两手扶着橄榄树，

But still felt weak and tired.

Esha questioned Nadi:
"You have eaten honey in nine caves
And had sour vines on nine mountains.
Why do you still feel weak?
Is it because you are pregnant?"
Nadi answered,
"I'm not pregnant.
I just want to eat sour things."

The fetus was growing bigger every day.
Soon the baby would be born,
But Nadi felt weak and tired.
How could she recover her strength?

She went to the valley,
Where she leant against
A loquat tree,
Which began to bear fruit.

Nadi went to the flat land,
Where she leant against

身子靠着橄榄树，
橄榄果儿结得更多了。

娜笛找到凹塘边，
两手扶着杨柳树，
身子靠着杨柳树，
杨柳像娜笛那样娇柔。

娜笛找到红靛，
孩子生到红靛林。
血染红了红靛叶，
血染红了红靛根。

厄莎算算时辰，
娜笛怀孕十个月，
胎儿应该降生。
厄莎看见娜笛，
娜笛脸色像朵白菌；
娜笛如实告诉厄莎，
胎儿已经降生。

孩子生了九双，
像小狗小猪一样，

An olive tree,
Which bore more fruit than ever.

Nadi went to the pond,
Where she leant against
A willow tree,
Which was as delicate as she.

Finally, Nadi went to the coleus wood,
Where she gave birth.
The leaves and the roots
Of the coleus were dyed red.

Esha reckoned that
The baby should be born now,
As Nadi had been pregnant for ten months.
He saw Nadi and found that
She looked as pale as a white mushroom.
Nadi told Esha the truth,
That the babies had been born.

There were nine pairs of them in all,
Like puppies or baby pigs,

多了抱不回来，
多了无法抚养。

厄莎唤来所有动物，
一齐来到厄莎住处。
大家静静地站着，
听候厄莎吩咐。

厄莎叫土蜂找小孩，
土蜂飞到九水汇合处。
土蜂找到了小孩，
但未告诉厄莎实话。
厄莎用金棍银棍打土蜂，
把土蜂的身子打成两截。
厄莎怜惜它死期未到，
忙用丝线把两截身子连上，
土蜂呵，
变成粗身、大肚、细细腰。

厄莎叫喜鹊去找小孩，
喜鹊飞到九水汇合处。
小孩找到了，
但未告诉厄莎实话。

Too many for Nadi to carry home,
Too many to be raised.

Esha called all the animals
To his place,
Where they stood quietly,
Waiting for his instructions.

Esha sent the wild bee to look for the babies.
The bee flew to where the nine rivers converged
And found the children,
But didn't tell Esha the truth.
Esha beat the bee with golden sticks and silver sticks,
Breaking its body in two.
Considering the bee was not doomed to die yet,
Esha linked the two parts with a silk thread.
Since then, the wild bee
Has always had a huge belly and a thin waist.

Esha sent the magpie to look for the babies.
It flew to where the nine rivers converged
And found the children.
But the magpie didn't tell Esha the truth.

厄莎处罚喜鹊：
不准喜鹊在高处搭窝，
不准喜鹊在低处搭窝。
喜鹊害怕厄莎，
自己住在半山垭。

厄莎叫酸蜂找小孩，
酸蜂飞到九水汇合处。
酸蜂认真找、仔细瞧，
有的孩子躺在河里静静睡，
有的孩子哇哇叫。

酸蜂转回来，
狂风吹起来，
可怜小小的酸蜂，
飞在科吉罗吉山上掉下来。
摔掉了酸蜂儿的牙齿，
摔伤了酸蜂儿的翅膀，
酸蜂儿没有呻吟，
歪歪倒倒站起来。
酸蜂儿走了九里，
酸蜂儿爬了九里，
历尽了千辛万苦，

Esha punished it
By not allowing it to build its nest
Either in a high place or in a low place.
The magpie dared not disobey Esha,
So it lived on the mountainside.

Esha sent the stingless bee to look for the babies.
It flew to where the nine rivers converged
And, looking carefully, found that
Some babies were sleeping quietly in the river,
Others were crying loudly.

On the way back,
There was a gale.
The poor little bee dropped down
When it was flying over Kejiluoji Mountain,
Breaking its teeth
And hurting its wings.
But the little bee struggled to its feet,
Without moaning or crying.
It walked nine miles
And crawled nine more,
Reaching Esha's house

终于爬进厄莎房里来。

厄莎眉开又眼笑，
直把酸蜂儿夸：
“酸蜂只有头发大，
风里雨里都不怕。
为人做了好事情，
子孙心中都记下。
给你头上放蜜，
给你脚上放蜜，
让你酿不完的蜜，
让你采不完的花。”

厄莎吩咐螃蟹，
叫它去捞小孩。
螃蟹捞起小孩，
动物把孩子送上晒台。
抬清水洗小孩，
用布把小孩包起来。
小孩放在晒台上，
放了长长一大排。
厄莎叫来动物，
要它们给小孩喂奶。

After overcoming a thousand hardships.

Esha was all smiles
And lavished praises upon the sour bee,
"The sour bee is as tiny as a hair,
But it braves gale and storm.
What it has done for human beings
Will be remembered by future generations.
I now anoint your head
And feet with honey,
Which means there will always be
Plenty of flowers for you to gather nectar."

Esha sent the crab
To get the babies out of water.
It did so.
Other animals took them to Esha's place,
Where they washed them with clean water,
Wrapped them up in cloth,
And laid them in a long row
On the veranda.
Esha had the animals come over
And feed the babies with their own milk.

狗来喂奶，
厄莎告诉小孩：
“长大不吃狗肉。”
牛来喂奶，
厄莎告诉小孩：
“长大不吃牛肉。”
猪来喂奶，
厄莎告诉小孩：
“长大不吃猪肉。”
……

十八个小孩，
一个吃一样奶，
以后便不能吃祖宗吃奶的动物，
这样规定流传到子孙后代。

孩子学会了走路，
孩子学会了说话，
就是没有名字，
称“你”、叫“他”，叽哩哇拉。
厄莎想了很久，
每个孩子都起一个名字：

The dog came to feed them.
Esha told the babies,
"Don't eat dog meat when you grow up."
The cow came to feed them.
Esha told the babies,
"Don't eat beef when you grow up."
The pig came to feed them.
Esha told the babies,
"Don't eat pork when you grow up."
…

The eighteen children
Drank different animals' milk.
It has since become a rule that later generations
Do not eat the animals that had fed their ancestors.

The children learnt to walk.
The children learnt to speak.
But as they had no names,
They were called "you", "he", whatever.
Esha pondered long and hard
And came up with a name for each child.

狗送回来的男孩叫扎丕，
女孩叫娜丕；
猪送回来的男孩叫扎娃，
女孩叫娜娃；
牛送回来的男孩叫扎努，
女孩叫娜努；
羊送回来的男孩叫扎药，
女孩叫娜药；
鸡送回来的男孩叫扎呵，
女孩叫娜呵；
马送回来的男孩叫扎母，
女孩叫娜母；
豹子送回来的男孩叫扎拉，
女孩叫娜拉；
猴子送回来的男孩叫扎莫，
女孩叫娜莫；
蛇送回来的男孩叫扎斯，
女孩叫娜斯。

后来又生兄妹俩，
领回的动物已经遗忘。
厄莎给他们起名扎倮、娜已，
叫他俩领导搞生产。

The boy brought back by the dog was called Zhapi,
And the girl was called Napi.
The boy brought back by the pig was called Zhawa,
And the girl was called Nawa.
The boy brought back by the cow was called Zhanu,
And the girl was called Nanu.
The boy brought back by the goat was called Zhayao,
And the girl was called Nayao.
The boy brought back by the chicken was called Zhahe,
And the girl was called Nahe.
The boy brought back by the horse was called Zhamu,
And the girl was called Namu.
The boy brought back by the leopard was called Zhala,
And the girl was called Nala.
The boy brought back by the monkey was called Zhamo,
And the girl was called Namo.
The boy brought back by the snake was called Zhasi,
And the girl was called Nasi.

Later one more brother and sister were born,
But Esha forgot which animal brought them back.
So he named them Zhaluo and Nayi respectively
And asked them to take charge of food production.

三　取火

九双孩子生在地上，
他们都不穿衣裳。
为了抵抗风寒，
个个都长了翅膀。
人们有了两只翅膀，
用一只当篾笆，
另一只当被子，
两只翅膀铺成一张床。

厄莎分出一点心，
放在高山头上，
突然一声雷响，
闪出万道金光。
火星飞到山坡上，
各种动物都来抢。
最先得火的是老鼠，
它把火种带到树上。

飞鼠原来没有翅膀，
老鼠想要人的翅膀，

III. Producing Fire

When the nine pairs of children were born,
They lay on the ground, with nothing on.
So they grew wings
To protect themselves from the cold.
As they each had two wings,
They used one as the mat
And the other as the quilt,
Making one bed.

Esha cut off a small piece of his heart
And put it on the top of the mountain.
Suddenly, there was a roar of thunder
And a thousand flashes of lightning,
Sending sparks all over the slope,
Which all the animals scrambled to collect.
The flying rat was the first to get a spark,
Which it took up a tree.

At the time, the flying rat was wingless.
It wanted men's wings

人也想要老鼠的火，
老鼠不敢和人来往，
人也不敢同老鼠商量。

尖嘴老鼠来说合，
尖嘴老鼠说：
“有了翅膀能在天上飞，
飞到树上有吃喝。”
尖嘴老鼠对人说：
“有了火种好做活，
发展生产有吃喝。”
人向老鼠换火种，
老鼠不愿换，
老鼠对人说：
“你不添点东西我不换。”
人添给老鼠力甫果，
老鼠同意了换火。
他们换得了火，
喜讯告诉厄莎。
厄莎告诉他们：
“你们换得火，
以后日子就会好过。”

And men wanted its spark.
The rat dared not have anything to do with men.
Men dared not talk with the rat, either.

The mouse came to mediate
Between the rat and men, saying,
"If you have wings, you can fly in the air
And eat a lot of good things on the trees."
Then the mouse said to men,
"If you have fire,
You can do things more easily
And produce more food to eat."
So men tried to barter wings for fire,
But the rat rejected them, saying,
"You must add something to it."
Men added some lifu fruit,
And the rat agreed.
Men got fire
And told Esha the good news.
Esha said,
"Now you have fire,
You will be better off."

他们高高兴兴去放火，
大火烧遍了山坡，
树木花草被烧死，
飞禽走兽无处躲。
大火越烧越旺，
他们急得去找厄莎。
厄莎用哈灭那[①]打出黑棉花，
厄莎用哈灭那打出白棉花。
黑棉花变成黑云，
白棉花变成白云；
黑云变成黑丝堆，
白云变成白丝堆。
黑云不会走，
白云不会走，
扎倮、娜已地边走几转，
黑云会走了，
白云翻滚滚。

太阳照着黑云，
黑云变成雨水；
太阳照着白云，
白云变成雨水。

---

① 哈灭那：一种土火炮。

Happily, men started a fire.
Unfortunately, it spread all over the slope,
Burning trees, flowers and grass,
Killing birds and animals.
The fire was burning more and more fiercely.
Men had to go to Esha for help,
Who shot his hamiena[①] to create black cotton,
Which turned into dark clouds.
He then created white cotton,
Which turned into white clouds.
But the dark clouds became a pile of black threads,
Unable to move.
The white clouds became a pile of white threads,
Unable to move.
So Zhaluo and Nayi
Paced around the field several times.
Then the clouds could float and roll.

The sun shone on the dark clouds,
Causing a heavy shower.
It shone on the white clouds,
Causing rain water to be released.

① Hamiena is a cannon.

雷声轰响，
风雨交加，
雨点鸡蛋大，
山梁山箐溅雨花。

风停了，
雨停了，
火熄了，
只有浓烟在缭绕。
浓烟求石头救命，
石头说：
“你是烟火，
不能在我身上藏躲。”

石头不肯救烟火，
蚯蚓来说合：
“你和烟火在一起，
风吹雨打你不怕，
千年万载更坚硬。”
烟火同石头结合，
从此石头有了火。

Thunder roared,
The wind blew,
Rain drops were as big as eggs,
Falling over hills and vales.

The wind stopped,
The rain ceased,
The fire went out,
There was only some lingering smoke,
Which asked a stone for help.
But the stone said,
"You may start a fire.
I can't hide you."

As the stone wouldn't save the smoke,
The earthworm tried to persuade it,
"If you and the smoke stay together,
You will fear neither wind nor rain,
And grow harder and harder with time."
So the stone accepted the smoke
And has produced fire with it ever since.

四　打猎

天上飞鸟在叫，
地上野兽在吼，
它们盯着扎笛、娜笛，
一心想吃人肉。

天上飞鸟在叫，
地上野兽在吼。
扎笛、娜笛吓得脸色发白，
想个法子赶走飞禽走兽。

厄莎知道扎笛、娜笛的心事，
叫来飞禽走兽。
厄莎对它们说：
“要吃扎笛、娜笛不难，
你们各自做好坑子、索扣……”
大鱼、小鱼做网，
小雀、大雀做扣，
老熊、豹子挖坑，
累得它们大汗直流。

IV. Hunting

Birds cried in the sky.
Beasts roared on land.
They both gazed at Zhadi and Nadi,
Yearning to eat their flesh.

Birds cried in the sky.
Beasts roared on land.
Zhadi and Nadi looked pale with fear.
They thought about how to drive the animals away.

Esha knew what they worried about.
He summoned the birds and beasts
And said to them,
"It's not difficult for you to eat Zhadi and Nadi.
Each of you dig a pit and make a snare…"
Thus the fish wove nets,
The birds made snares,
And the bear and the leopard dug pits.
All of them were tired and sweating.

网做好了，
扣做好了，
坑挖好了。
厄莎告诉它们，
统统跟着我走，
要把胆子放大。

飞禽淌着口水，
走兽掉着舌头，
它们信步走着，
一心想吃人肉。

它们绕过山梁，
它们窜进夹沟，
突然听到人声大吼，
吓得它们惊慌逃走。
鱼儿钻进网里，
飞禽碰上扣子，
走兽陷进坑里，
自己把自己害死。

九对孩子长大了，
每对又生了九百个孩子。

When the nets had been woven,
The snares had been made,
And the pitfalls had been dug,
Esha told them
To follow him
As boldly as they could.

They followed him, as they were told,
The mouths of the birds watering,
The tongues of the beasts were sticking out,
Longing for human flesh.

They were passing the ridges
And entering deep valleys
When they heard men shouting loudly.
They panicked and fled in chaos.
The fish went into the nets,
The birds triggered the snares
And the beasts fell into the pits.
They brought about their own doom.

When the nine pairs of children grew up,
Each couple bore nine hundred children.

九百人住一个箐沟，
九百人住一匹梁子。
九百人吃光了甲哈草，
九百人啃缺了梁子。
他们转遍了深山，
他们转遍了坝子。
他们看到豹子、麂子肥又壮，
想要打死豹子、麂子。

他们做了套绳、标枪，
他们带上黄狗、黑狗，
他们追赶豹子、麂子，
一心要打死豹子、麂子。

九百人追赶，
足足追了三年，
豹子已经老了，
赶到水塘打死了豹子——
九百人投出标枪，
九百支标枪戳到豹子身上，
豹子倒在地上，
豹子的鲜血像溪水一样流淌。

Nine hundred people lived in one valley.
Another nine hundred lived on one ridge.
Nine hundred people ate up the jiaha grass.
Another nine hundred bit into the ridge.
They went into all the mountains.
They roamed over all the plains.
Seeing that the leopard and muntjac were fat,
They wanted to kill them.

They made snares and spears,
Took their yellow dog and black dog along,
And tracked the leopard and the muntjac down,
Determined to kill them.

Nine hundred people followed the animals
For three long years.
When the leopard was old,
They chased it into a pond and killed it.
They threw nine hundred spears,
Which all hit the leopard.
The animal fell to the ground,
Its blood running like a brook.

拿黄壶壶装豹血，
用甜紫檀木做壶塞，
用苦紫檀木做壶塞，
甜的那壶是甜血，
苦的那壶是苦血。

九百人将豹子抬回来，
把豹子放在厄莎的晒台。
九百人用扫把草叶剥皮，
九百人用石斧、竹刀割肉。

九百人站成九行，
九行分成九种民族。
厄莎站在中间，
给九个民族分肉。

有一个人站在火塘边，
慢慢烤了吃，
吃着嘴里说：
“瓦瓦来搞掌。”
这个人的子孙
就是拉祜族。

They used yellow jars to hold the leopard blood,
With sweet sandalwood
And bitter sandalwood as the corks.
The jar with the sweet cork held sweet blood.
The one with the bitter cork held bitter blood.

The nine hundred people carried the leopard
To Esha's house and put it on the veranda.
They peeled its skin with brooms and grass,
And cut its meat with stone axes and bamboo knives.

The nine hundred people stood in nine lines,
Symbolizing nine ethnic groups.
Esha stood in the middle
And distributed the leopard meat among them.

One man stood by the fire
And slowly roasted the meat.
As he ate the meat, he said something like
"Wa wa lai gao zhang".
His descendants
Would be the Lahu people.

有一个人煮来吃，
豹肉连汤一起吃，
吃着嘴里说：
“呼呼来底掌。”
这个人的子孙
就是佤族。

有一个人蹲在火塘旁边烧，
烧煳的豹肉味道苦，
吃着嘴里说：
“卡够来底掌。”
这个人的子孙
就是倭尼族。

有一个人刮洗了豹肉，
放在锅里煮熟吃，
吃着嘴里说：
“海歇辣掌。”
这个人的子孙
就是汉族。

有一个人煮了吃，

Another man stewed it
And ate both the meat and the soup,
Saying something like
“Hu hu lai di zhang”.
His descendants
Would be the Wa people.

Still another man squatted on the ground
And roasted the meat in the fire pit.
The burnt meat tasted bitter.
As he ate the meat, he said something like
“Ka gou lai di zhang”.
His descendants
Would be the Aini people.

A fourth man washed the meat
And cooked it in a pot.
As he ate the meat, he said something like
“Hai xie la zhang”.
His descendants
Would be the Han people.

A fifth man also stewed the meat.

埋头吃肉不说话。
这个人的子孙
就是老缅族。

有一个人分到一块肉，
这块肉上有伤口，
不生不熟烧来吃，
吃着嘴里说：
“杀区底吐巧学罗。”
这个人的子孙
就是傣族。

民族分出来了，
厄莎分住处。
鸭子领着傣族到水边，
傣族就在水边住。
喜鹊领着汉族走到半山腰，
汉族就在山腰住。
佤族跟着白鹇走，
大山头上佤族住。
拉祜跟着骆驼鸟走，
山梁子上拉祜住。

He ate it silently.
His descendants
Would be the Bamar people.

Another man got a piece of meat
That had a cut in it.
He roasted it half raw.
As he ate the meat, he said something like
"Sha qu di tu qiao xue luo".
His descendants
Would be the Dai people.

Now that the ethnic groups had been named,
Esha assigned them to different living areas.
The duck led the Dai to the riverside,
Where they would reside.
The magpie led the Han to the mountainside,
Where they would live.
The Wa followed the silver pheasant
To live on the top of the mountain.
The Lahu followed the ostrich to the ridges,
Where they would live.

各民族有了住处，
人人喜喜欢欢，
像兄弟姐妹一样，
不分什么界限。

五　分配

各族有了住处，
住了九年时间，
住满了三架梁子，
住满了三个凹子。

扎倮、娜已兄妹俩，
领着大家搞生产。
挑菜、挖蜜、打猎，
天亮忙到天黑。

早上找到阿戈山，
晚上找上阿沃山。
大橙树下九窝蜂，
蜂窝里面做满了蜜。
扎倮、娜已掏来蜜，
一人一份大家吃。

All the ethnic groups had an area to live in.
Everybody was happy.
They got on very well,
Like brothers and sisters.

V. Distribution of Food

Every ethnic group had an area to inhabit.
After nine years,
They had occupied three mountains
And three valleys.

Zhaluo and Nayi
Led the others in food production,
Busy picking wild vegetables, digging for honey,
And hunting from dawn to dusk.

At dawn they searched Age Mountain.
At dusk they arrived at Awo Mountain.
Under a huge orange tree,
They found nine hives full of honey,
Which they gathered
And distributed to everybody.

娜已打了一只鹿，
分成九份血，
分成九份肉，
一个民族一壶血，
一个民族一份肉。

扎倮打死一只豪猪，
豪猪分成九份。
娜已那份少，
只有一条尾巴根。

娜已嫌尾巴太少，
埋怨扎倮太不公平。
妹妹带着女人走河尾，
哥哥领着男人走河头。
兄妹二人各走各的路，
郁郁闷闷不快乐。

兄妹走到半路上，
看见蚂蚁在运粮，
大家不分男和女，
齐齐整整排成行。

Nayi killed a deer
And divided its blood and meat
Into nine shares.
Each ethnic group got one jar of blood
And one share of meat.

Zhaluo killed a porcupine,
Which was divided into nine shares, too.
Nayi got the smallest share,
Just a tail.

Nayi complained that
Zhaluo was unfair.
She led the women to the lower reaches of the river,
While Zhaluo led the men to the upper reaches.
The brother and sister went their own way,
Feeling depressed and unhappy.

On their way, they saw ants
Carrying food home.
All the ants, both male and female,
Worked in neat lines.

妹妹看见蚂蚁，
想起哥哥心寒；
哥哥看见蚂蚁，
想起妹妹孤单。

妹妹打水到井边，
看到金竹一片，
想到会做响篾的哥哥，
哥哥的身影就在水里出现。

哥哥拿来干牛粪，
烧起白生生的浓烟。
妹妹闻到烟味，
知道是哥哥把她呼唤。
哥哥住在杜拉洛拉卡密，
妹妹找到杜拉洛拉卡密。
哥哥把响篾丢到井边，
妹妹走到井边就把响篾弹。
哥哥认出是妹妹来了，
他双脚蹦跳心喜欢。

When the sister saw this,
She thought of her brother's disappointment.
When the brother saw this,
He thought of his sister's loneliness.

When the sister went to the well to fetch water,
She saw a golden bamboo forest, which reminded her
Of her brother making the jaw harp.
Suddenly, her brother's image appeared in the water.

The brother made a fire with dried cow dung,
Which sent heavy white smoke into the air.
The sister smelled the smoke
And knew that her brother was calling her.
Her brother lived in Dulaluolakami.
So she went there to look for him.
The brother left a jaw harp by the well.
The sister picked it up and began to play it.
Knowing that it was his sister,
The brother jumped for joy.

六　盖房子

喜鹊有自己的巢，
老鼠有自己的窝，
人们无房子住，
真是不好过。

扎倮、娜已转到高山上，
扎倮、娜已转到坝子里，
白天黑夜砍树木，
白天黑夜砍竹子。
砍下树木几大堆，
砍下竹子几大堆。

树木晒了七天七夜，
竹子晒了七天七夜，
树木竹子晒干了，
老老小小一起盖新房。

栗树做柱，
水冬瓜树做梁，
荒地树做牵手，

VI. Building Houses

The magpie had its nest.
The rat had its nest, too.
Without houses,
Humans had a hard time.

Zhaluo and Nayi went to the mountains,
Zhaluo and Nayi went to the flatlands.
They cut trees day and night,
They cut bamboos day and night.
They cut several huge piles of trees,
They cut several huge piles of bamboos.

They dried the trees and bamboos in the sun
For seven days and nights.
When these materials were dried,
All began to build new houses together.

They used chestnut trees as pillars,
Alder trees as beams,
Wasteland trees as purlins,

茅草盖房顶，
破好竹子编墙。
盖出新房四个角，
新房大门朝太阳。

新房盖好了，
大家喜洋洋。
娜已又在阿戈山开沟，
扎倮又在阿沃山开田，
丘丘田块像叶子，
弯弯曲曲的水沟绕过山。

七　造农具

大土蜂从麻栗树上飞过，
人们在后面紧紧追着。
土蜂飞过勐薄坝，
土蜂飞过白吉流村，
蜂儿越飞越高，
人们想追追不着。
土蜂飞过冬瓜树林，
土蜂飞过绿树林，
飞到勐谷坝尾山梁上，

Cogon grass to thatch the roofs,
And bamboo strips to weave walls.
The new houses had four corners
With the front gates facing the rising sun.

All were happy
When the new houses had been completed.
Then Nayi dug a water channel on Age Mountain,
Which zigzagged on the slope.
Zhaluo built rice fields on Awo Mountain,
Which looked like leaves patched together.

VII. Making Farm Tools

The wild bees flew over the teak trees,
Followed closely by people looking for honey.
The bees crossed the Mengbo Plain
And Baijiliu Village,
Flying higher and higher,
Leaving the hunters far behind.
They flew over a donggua wood,
They flew over a green forest.
They reached the ridge near the Menggu Plain,

大群土蜂进了蜂窝门。
大伙约着烧土蜂，
一烧烧了四个月，
蜂窝越烧越红，
洞子里像羊头淌出羊血。

土蜂早已烘死了，
蜂洞的火不熄，
原来不是羊血，
是铁娘子流出的鲜血。

马鹿朝前跪着，
一个蚊子飞来咬一口，
马鹿一蹦跳，
撞倒朱栗碰断角。
人们拾回马鹿角，
马鹿角有三叉，
大家用来挖铁矿，
又尖又硬力量大。

铁矿挖出来一大堆，
炼铁没有炭。

And entered their hive in a hole.
The people decided to get them out using fire,
Which lasted four months.
The hive was burning hot,
Like a goat shedding blood.

The bees had long been dead,
But the fire was still burning in the hole.
It was not goat blood, they found,
But Lady Iron was bleeding.[1]

The red deer knelt on its front legs
When a mosquito gave it a bite.
The deer jumped up with a start,
Bumped into a chestnut tree and broke its antlers,
Which the people picked up and brought back home.
As the antlers had three forks
And were pointed, hard and powerful,
They used them to mine iron ore.

They dug up a huge pile of iron ore,
But they needed charcoal to smelt it.

① It means iron ore was burning inside the hive. – Translator's note

扎保、娜已转到坝子看，
砍倒椎栗来烧炭。
炭火烧得旺，
铁水往外淌，
铁水凝成粑，
就像牛屎块。

找来铁匠泥梭[1]人，
找来麝身当风箱。
麝毛变成风板，
麝尾变成炉杆，
麝手变成钳子，
麝脚变成大锤，
麝头变成砧。
照着白花果一样，
打出第一把芟刀；
照着推屎虫一样，
打出第一个犁头。
犁头犁地土翻浪，
芟刀芟草闪闪亮。
拉祜有了犁头、芟刀，
生产好搞了。

---

① 泥梭：地名。

Zhaluo and Nayi went to the flatland
And cut down chestnut trees to make charcoal.
The charcoal fire was burning merrily;
Molten iron flowed out.
When cooled, it became chunks
Like pieces of cow dung.

They sent for the smith in Nisuo[1].
They used the body of a musk deer as bellows,
Its fur as a wind board,
Its tail as a stove pole,
Its front paws as pliers,
Its legs as hammers,
And its head as an anvil.
Using the Japanese ternstroemia as a model,
They forged the first sickle.
Using the dung beetle as a model,
They made the first plough.
When it was plowed, the soil turned like waves.
When cutting grass, the sickle shone like light.
When the Lahu had these tools,
Farming was much easier than ever.

① Nisuo is a place.

八　种谷子

厄莎的姑娘正在舂米，
簸米时掉下一颗谷子，
斑鸠衔了谷子，
飞到太阳里，
飞到云彩里。

扎倮、娜已没有种子，
不能种田种地。
他们去问厄莎，
厄莎说："种子被斑鸠含去。"
三天三夜之后，
斑鸠到野水塘喝水，
扎倮、娜已用扣绳把它套住。

剥开斑鸠嗉袋，
找到一粒种籽。
扎倮、娜已嫌种籽太少，
厄莎说：
"一粒下地收万粒。
田谷种在水田里，

VIII. Growing Rice

Esha's daughter was husking rice.
When she fanned the chaff,
The only unhusked grain of rice fell to the ground.
A turtledove picked it up
And flew into the cloudy sky.

Without rice seeds,
Zhaluo and Nayi couldn't grow anything.
So they went to ask Esha for help.
But Esha said, "It has been stolen by the turtledove."
Three days and three nights later,
When the turtledove was drinking water from a pond,
Zhaluo and Nayi caught it in a snare.

They opened the turtledove's stomach
And found a grain of seed,
Which they thought too little.
But Esha said,
"Sow one grain and you'll harvest ten thousand.
Paddy rice is grown in irrigated fields.

旱谷种在山坡地。”

二月到来了，
要去撒谷种，
田谷种送到田里，
旱谷种送到地里。
田地有塘子，
种子撒在塘子里。

田头种糯谷，
田尾种饭谷，
谷子长不出来，
几乎要绝种。

田头种饭谷，
田尾种糯谷，
谷子长出来，
像法老草又粗又壮。

三月到来了，
田里出秧苗。
四月五月到，

Upland rice is grown in dry soil."

When February[①] came,
It was time to scatter the rice seeds
In the little pools
In both the paddy fields in the flatlands
And the dry soil on the slope
To cultivate seedlings.

They planted sticky rice in the upper parts of the fields,
And sowed nonsticky rice in the lower parts of the fields,
But the rice couldn't grow,
Leaving no grains of seed to reproduce.

Then they planted nonsticky rice in the upper parts
And sticky rice in the lower parts.
Now the rice grew well,
Its plants as strong as the falao grass.

When March came,
Rice seedlings emerged in the fields.
In April and May,

① The months in this book refer to lunar months. – Translator's note

田里除杂草，
薅秧要薅好。

六月到来了，
秧苗发青了。
发青不打苞，
蜻蜓田上飞，
秧苗怀胎了。
秧苗出穗了，
不会开花儿，
找来厄莎的金花，
找来厄莎的银花。
谷子有花了，
谷子出穗了。
谷子有穗不会饱，
露水田上洒，
谷子长浆饱满了，
串串谷穗弯下腰。

七月日子到，
谷子成熟了，
田里黄金金，
田边小雀叫。

Zhaluo and Nayi were busy weeding the fields
And thinning out the seedlings.

When June came,
The seedlings turned dark green.
Before they budded,
When dragonflies flew about over the fields,
The seedlings were pollinated.
Then the ears started to appear,
But they did not blossom.
Zhaluo and Nayi got gold flowers
And silver flowers from Esha.
The seedlings blossomed,
The seedlings produced ears.
Yet the grain did not grow full.
When they splashed dew water in the fields,
The rice grains grew full
And the spikes bent low.

July was the month
When the rice ripened.
The fields turned golden.
Sparrows sang happily.

搭起窝棚来，
拉起篾索吆，
认真赶小雀，
谷子保护好。

八月到来了，
谷子熟透了。
女人用镰刀割谷子，
用弯勾、篾笆打谷子；
男人编篾篓，
用篾篓背谷子。
男人背上背谷子，
女人头上背谷子。
谷子背回家，
倒在碓窝里，
杵棒重重舂，
分成糠和米。
男人编簸箕，
女人来簸米，
隔开了糠秕，
谷子变成米。

Zhaluo and Nayi set up sheds in the fields
And stayed there during the day
To protect the rice from the birds
By frightening them away with a bamboo rope.

When August came,
The rice was ready to be harvested.
The women reaped it with sickles
And husked it with sticks and bamboo mats.
The men wove baskets
For carrying the rice.
Men carried the baskets on their backs,
While women carried them on their heads.
They carried the rice home
And put it in a stone mortar.
Then they pestled it hard
To husk it.
The men wove winnowing baskets,
The women winnowed the rice,
Blowing the chaff away,
Leaving the husked rice.

新米白亮亮，
土锅放在三脚上；
炉塘火苗哈哈笑，
煮出饭来喷喷香。

九　种棉花

忙着到北京，
带回棉花籽。
带着种籽到河边，
白花树下忙芟地。

地芟好了，
草晒干了，
放火烧干草，
翻松土地种棉花。

棉花长出来，
大家忙锄草，
收回雪白的棉花，
用轧花机压成软软的花絮。

纺好线，织好布，

The new rice was white and bright.
A pot was placed on a tripod.
The flames in the fire pit were laughing loudly.
The rice in the pot was irresistibly fragrant.

IX. Growing Cotton

The couple went to Beijing
And brought back cotton seeds.
They took the seeds to the riverbank
And cut the grass under the white flower tree.

After they cut all the grass,
Dried it, and burned it,
They prepared the land
For planting cotton.

When the cotton grew up,
They weeded the fields.
In time, they harvested snow-white cotton
And removed the seeds with a cotton gin.

They spun the cotton, wove cloth,

染上颜色做衣服。
黑衣裳，花衣裳，
长短大小各自做。

谷子收到家，
家家又织布。
有穿要勤，
有吃要做。
年年月月，
厄莎和他的子孙，
上山打猎不怕豹子咬，
下地做活不怕冷和热。

十　鹌鹑跳舞

拉祜的节日，
厄莎定在正月初一。
节日有了，
过年期到了，
男人做芦笙，
姑娘做响篾。
寨头寨尾都来跳舞，
熙熙攘攘闹闹热热。

And dyed it for sewing clothes
In all kinds of colors
And different sizes, as they liked.

As soon as the rice was harvested,
The families were busy weaving cloth.
Their industriousness gave them enough to wear.
Diligence provided them with enough to eat.
Year after year, and month after month,
Esha and his descendants
Went hunting without fearing leopards,
And tilled the land whether it was hot or cold.

X. Quail Dancing

Esha decided that the Lahu's festival
Would fall on the first day of January.
That was it.
When the day came,
The men made the lusheng,
The girls made the jaw harp.
All the villagers gathered to dance.
It was all hustle and bustle.

人们不会跳舞，
鹌鹑带着跳，
舞步轻盈，
姿态万千，
孔雀看了生嫉妒。
鹌鹑站在第一列，
孔雀站在第二列，
人们站在第三列，
越跳人越多，
歌儿越唱越热烈。
唱得夜哇子鸟嗓子哑，
杜鹃鸟儿嘴啼血。

鹌鹑尾巴三丈长，
翎毛摆动宝光闪，
它教大家跳又唱，
七天七夜心不烦。
孔雀尾巴光秃秃，
羽毛暗淡不好看，
心中打下坏主意，
跳舞场上它捣乱：
鹌鹑前面跳，
它在后面踩，

The people didn't know how to dance,
So the quail taught them.
It danced so lightly and gracefully
That the peacock was envious.
The quail stood in the first row,
The peacock stood in the second,
And the people stood in the third.
More and more people joined in.
The songs became louder and louder.
The birds sang so hard that
The night heron's voice became hoarse
And the nightingale's mouth started to bleed.

The quail's tail was ten meters long,
With feathers glistening like precious stones as it waved.
The quail taught the people to dance and sing,
For seven days and nights without feeling bored.
The peacock had a bare tail,
With feathers both dull and ugly.
Harboring ill feelings,
It made trouble during the dance.
As the quail danced ahead,
The peacock trod on its tail

跳了九十九步，
踩掉鹌鹑九十九支翎子。
舞蹈完了，
鹌鹑尾巴秃了，
孔雀换上鹌鹑的尾巴，
得意洋洋飞跑了。

跳了七天七夜，
歌唱完了，
舞跳完了。
家中鸡猪马牛无人管，
跑到深山野林去了。
男人抬着弓弩，
上山追赶打猎去了。

Ninety-nine times
And the quail lost ninety-nine plumes.
When the dance was over,
The quail had a bare tail.
The peacock put on the quail's plumes
And flew off proudly.

After seven days and nights,
The singing was over.
The dancing stopped.
While the people were enjoying themselves,
Their livestock ran off into the forest.
The men took up their bows and arrows
And went hunting the escaped animals.

歌尾

Epilogue

一年三百六十天，
今天是过年，
一年一次大节，
一年一次大团圆。
桃子花开了，
李子花开了，
春意最浓最艳，
最好日子是今天。

男的跳舞站中间，
女的跳舞围外面；
女的拍手银镯叮当响，
男的吹笙心儿欢。
跳吧！
唱吧！
让我们忘却一年的辛苦，
让我们送走过去的灾难。
打响哈灭那——
使我们精神振奋，
赶走邪魔保平安。

There are three hundred and sixty days in a year.
Today is New Year's Day,
The annual grand festival
For the annual grand reunion.
The peach trees are in blossom,
The plum trees are in blossom,
Spring is much in the air,
And today it is most fair.

The men dance in the middle,
The women dance in an outer ring.
The women clap their hands, their bracelets tinkling.
The men play the lusheng, their hearts filled with joy.
Oh, dance!
Oh, sing!
Let's forget the hard work of the year.
Let's drive off the misfortunes of the past.
Let's fire the hamiena –
To inspire ourselves and to ensure peace
By exorcising evil spirits.

我们围住温暖的火塘，
高高兴兴好过年，
喝足多依酒，
吃饱白米饭。

大年过完了，
各自回家了，
扛起犁头背起茇刀，
上山、下箐搞生产。

We gather around the fire pit
And celebrate the New Year.
We drink the duoyi wine to satisfaction,
We eat white rice until we are full.

When the festival activities are over,
Everybody goes home.
Taking up our plows and sickles,
We go and work on the hills and in the vales.

译后记

《牡帕密帕》是拉祜族民间流传最广的一部长篇诗体创世神话，流传于云南省普洱市澜沧拉祜族自治县境内，叙述厄莎天神造天地日月、造万物和人类以及人类初始阶段的生存状况等。

作为拉祜族人民传承历史悠久的口述文学精品，《牡帕密帕》具有很高的研究价值。2006年5月20日，云南省思茅市申报的《牡帕密帕》经国务院批准列入第一批国家级非物质文化遗产名录。

《牡帕密帕》有不同版本，但故事基本大同小异。此次英译采用的源文本是刘辉豪先生整理、云南人民出版社1979年出版的汉语版《牡帕密帕》，包括以下内容：歌头；第一章　造天造地；第二章　造物造人；第三章　生活下去；歌尾。其中第三章又分为十节：一　扎笛、娜笛结婚；二　第一代人；三　取火；四　打猎；五　分配；六　盖房子；七　造农具；八　种谷子；九　种棉花；十　鹌鹑跳舞。

在动笔翻译之前，译者拜访了原文整理者刘辉豪先生，请他为英译授权，刘先生爽快地答应了译者的请求，译者深表谢忱。由于刘先生年事已高，译者没有就诗的内容向他请教。在翻译过程中，为了准确理解诗中所涉及的拉祜族文化知识，译者查阅了大量的相关文献资料，前往云南澜沧拉祜族自治县实地考察了拉祜族的房屋建筑结构，并就有关问题请教了昆明医科大学的张宏斌教授和普洱学院的王江华教授，获益良多，译者在此一并表示感谢。

李昌银

Translator's Afterword

Mupamipa is the most popular creation epic of the Lahu people, circulating mainly in Lancang Lahu Autonomous County, Yunnan, China. It tells the story of how God Esha created the sky, the earth, the moon, the stars, and all other things, including human beings, and how mankind lived in their early days.

As a surviving epic in the oral tradition of the Lahu people, *Mupamipa* is an important text for people interested in the ethnic groups of Yunnan in general and in Lahu history and culture in particular. Its great value is testified by the fact that it was listed in the first national catalog of intangible cultural heritage created by the State Council in 2006.

The story exists in different forms, but the basic plot is the same. This version, edited by Mr. Liu Huihao and published in August, 1979 by Yunnan People's Publishing House, contains the following parts: Prologue; Canto 1 Creation of the Sky and the Earth; Canto 2 Creation of Nature and Human Beings; Canto 3 Survival, which includes: Ⅰ. Zhadi and Nadi Getting Married, Ⅱ. The First Generation of Humans, Ⅲ. Producing Fire, Ⅳ. Hunting, Ⅴ. Distribution of Food, Ⅵ. Building Houses, Ⅶ. Making Farm Tools, Ⅷ. Growing Rice, Ⅸ. Growing Cotton, Ⅹ.

Quail Dancing; and Epilogue.

Before starting the translation, I visited Mr. Liu Huihao, the editor of the poem, and asked him for permission to translate it into English. He graciously granted my request, for which I'm very grateful. As he is 87 years old, I didn't bother him with questions about the poem. When translating this poem, I read a lot of literature on the story and its historical context in order to acquaint myself with the Lahu culture in the poem. I also went to the Lancang Lahu Autonomous County to examine the style of the house structure of the Lahu people and discussed Lahu architecture with Professor Zhang Hongbin of Kunming Medical University and Professor Wang Jianghua of Pu'er University. Both of them are familiar with the Lahu culture. Here I would like to thank them for sharing what they knew with me.

Li Changyin

译者简介

李昌银，云南师范大学外国语学院教授。近年来发表有关英语教学、翻译研究与文学批评方面的论文30余篇，主持完成2008年国家社科基金西南边疆课题1项。研究兴趣：后殖民文学、现代性与翻译。

About the Translator

Li Changyin is a professor of English in the School of Foreign Languages and Literature at Yunnan Normal University, Kunming, China. In recent years, he has published about thirty articles on English teaching, translation and literature. He is the Principal Investigator of a project sponsored in 2008 by the National Social Science Fund of China. His current research interests cover postcolonial literature, modernity and translation.